I0772397

CLARITY'S DAWN

THE SKYWARD SAGA
BOOK 3

A.R. KNIGHT

My home appears from nothing in the dark. A great brown and white circle hanging against an endless black expanse with bright lights twinkling, like holes in a leafy canopy. I stare at it through the front windshield of the shuttle, my mouth open. My eyes blink and see that my home is still there. When I left it, when I'd been taken from it, I thought I would never see its jungles, its oceans and mountains again. I thought my family, all that I knew, was lost forever.

Yet here it is again.

Are you happy?

Ignos, who I once thought was a god, what is now a strange creature living inside of me, sends its words in the same way I might think them. Wisps of feeling, images and emotion passing through me. Am I happy?

Yes.

The shuttle will guide itself. Take in the view. Relax.

I don't have much choice anyway. The bands locking around my feet and the netting clinging to my back, the things that kept me stable during the leap, do not retract. I'm stuck, as are my two friends, Viera and Malo, behind me. That might be a problem if we had anywhere to go, but right now we're transfixed by what's going on in front of us.

The brown circle is growing larger, closer. In between the drifts of white, which Ignos tells me are clouds, I see black specks cut across the view. Some larger than others, some appearing, like the birds of my home, to fly in formation.

Are they others? New Oratus, new creatures coming to take me away as soon as I land?

No. Those are my friends.

Ignos had mentioned, when I first found it in that crashed rock months ago, that its friends would follow. Its job was to prep Earth for them. These other gods would rescue us from hardship. Solve our problems and bring us to a new era of happiness and peace.

So why, why does this strange knot start to form in my stomach as I stare at the growing brown mass. As the specks define themselves into strange shapes. Some, like the planet, are circular. Others are jagged, made of lines and cutting edges as they zip around.

"Whatever those are, they're coming closer," Viera says.

She's speaking about a set of three things off to our left. I can see them because, from the twin wings on their sides, bright red lights glow towards us.

"I can't move," Malo adds. "Can you, Kaishi? Can you free us?"

I ask Ignos the question, but the creature doesn't respond. It's staying silent now, and my unease grows. "I don't know how."

"Better hope these are friends, or we're in trouble," Viera says.

"Ignos says they are."

"Forgive me if I don't trust that thing."

I watch as the three ships outside slide around us. To the point where, when the ships leave my view, I can still see the slight glow of those red points. The world in front of us has grown to fill the visible space. Parts of the brown shade differently. Large circles. Ripples in the earth, which I assume must be mountains. Others look like deep divots. Craters, perhaps.

What I don't see are jungles. What I don't see are oceans.

Are they on the other side?

Ignos doesn't answer. The shuttle begins to shake, and suddenly the edges, then the entire windshield glows white and orange and red.

"What's going on?" Malo says. "Is Ignos telling you anything?"

Everything will be fine.

Ignos' words carry condescension, the same sort of kind dismissal that my parents used to give me when I was small child. An answer that says Ignos does not trust me with more.

As quickly as the fire picks up it recedes, and now icy particles begin to form. Strange crystalline formations grow on the glass. From hot to cold to melting again almost as soon as they form. All I see now is foggy gray white.

"I don't know what's happening," I say.

"That makes three of us," Viera replies.

In a past life, before, I would've prayed. Prayed to Ignos, the real god, not the creature, to deliver me from harm. And for the first time since that strange night in the dark jungle when I saw the ship that bore this creature to me, I pray. Pray to a god I no longer think is inside me, one that I hope is around me. Is guiding me.

Malo hears my words and joins in. It's a simple, common ritual. An ask for forgiveness, for courage, for guidance. For protection and love.

"Here's hoping that works," Viera says when we're done; the Lunare doesn't join us in the prayer but she's happy to reap the benefits of it.

For a moment, it seems like we do. The gray breaks and beneath us I see something I can recognize; the tall spire, snow-tipped, of a mountain. Though this one, unlike the rocky gray against the green jungles of my home is almost all black. Around it, at its base and stretching for as far as I can see, there is no green. Only whites and grays and blues and reds. Only buildings. Arcing and toppling on top of one another, stacked and merging. Split by long cylindrical tubes that circle and divide them like veins on a fern frond.

The knot in my stomach grows to full panic. Because I know now.

This is not my home.

The shuttle drops lower. We swoop along the mountain, and in the shimmering reflections of the tall buildings I can see that we are still being followed, tailed by the three craft that met us above the sky. But these are not the only things joining us in the air. Whereas my skies were filled with birds, these are full of objects of all sizes. They zip and dart everywhere, filling the blank spaces the same way fog or locusts might at home. I don't understand how none of them hit each other, and Ignos replies with a single word:

Automatic.

I don't know what it means. I don't know what any of this is. I don't understand what I see as I look inside the buildings that we pass, filled with strange devices, odd pink and yellow lights. Wide halls with groups of creatures I could never before imagine standing or moving. Talking or, in some cases, appearing to fire strange weapons like the kind the Oratus had on *Cobalt*.

Beneath us, the tubes seem to split everything, I see more shapes, several that look like Coorvin, the furry and big-eyed guide we'd left on the station. Called a Flaum, I think.

Below us, the travelers rocket by in small pods, sitting as they're shot along to whatever end. Beneath them, on the surface, there are red-lined roads. Paved in stone. Red brick that appears molded without crease. Walking feet, claws, or stranger things cover the surface as hordes of creatures meander back and forth. It's a sight that should fill me with wonder but instead twists me with dread.

"Where are we?" Malo says. "This isn't home."

No, it isn't.

I ask Ignos if it lied to me.

I never did. I let you assume. If you went back home now, the Oratus would simply take you again. I can't let that happen. I can't let you fall into their hands.

What I do is my choice.

No. Not anymore.

The shuttle takes a sharp right turn, coasting us above a broader avenue and underneath a series of archways that glow red as we pass beneath them. The ones in front shimmer a pale yellow, the same that I've seen on insects warning you not to get too close. I realize these arches are guiding us down, towards a wide gaping hole that appears to lead into the ground.

"Don't know what that thing inside your head is telling you, Kaishi," Viera says. "But I'm not inclined to trust a word it's saying. Wherever this is, it's not home. Whatever these things are, I'm betting they're not our friends."

"We can't do anything now," I say. "Look and learn. Try not to panic."

You can accept it. You can understand that your place in a larger galaxy is here. With us.

My place is with my people.

Kaishi, you have no people. All you have is me. All you have is what the Sevora will give you.

As I look forward, as we dive through the last of the arches and into an all-consuming dark beneath the ground, the only thing that breaks the mind-numbing shock is the cool wet of tears.

2 / FREE FLOATING

Time is a fluid concept. For Sax, at least, the definition of passing events is constantly in flux. Local time, measured by wherever he just happens to be. Galactic time, long ago shifting to measurements in cycles, grand events marking shifts in civilization's power and goals. And, of course, his own biology. The rate of cellular decay and regeneration in his muscles and tendons and organs. This last is most apparent to him now, sitting cramped with Bas, his pair, and the old speckle-furred Flaum Coorvin in an evac mod hurtling through space.

They've been busy, with Sax and Bas claiming all the healing ointments in the mod. Coorvin, using skills learned caring for Dalachite's many needs, has been stitching the two Oratus back together, salving burns and removing what doesn't heal for what can. The time passes in an itchy haze, with Sax's strength creeping back, though he has nowhere to use it, to test himself. The prospect, to come so far back and have no way to prove it, makes his tail twitch.

"Do you know what it would mean for us to die out here?" Sax hisses all of a sudden.

He does this more to break the silence, one that's been steadily growing in the eternity since they've launched from *Cobalt*. Since they've escaped from a space station hurtling towards its own ruin, whether by rogue asteroid or by internal power failures.

"I believe, in an environment such as this, were our bodies to fail we would drift, largely preserved, for a long while," Coorvin muses, his large black eyes staring off at nothing. "I don't believe there's enough biological matter in here for us to decay properly."

"Exactly," Sax says, though that's not at all what he meant, but it fits anyway. "We would lose our chance at honor. At victory. At solving the reason why."

"Why?" Bas hisses a lighter, cleaner note than Sax.

Like most things between the two, Bas is better, more beautiful.

"Because we don't know yet. We don't know why that Amigga cared so much about the humans. I don't know why fassoths were on the human's planet or how the technology we saw there came to exist. Its relation to the primitive structures is all wrong."

"An inquisitive Oratus?" Coorvin says. "I thought all of your kind were brutes. Bred for war and nothing else."

"I was," Sax says. He looks at his claws, the gray scales bleeding back from translucent pink and gray points. Four of them, one set on each arm, and two more talons on each of his thick legs, currently tucked in beneath him along with his tail. "I deserve to be in the midst of the enemy, tearing and shredding and slashing. Yet here I am sitting in this cramped prison waiting to die. Such a space makes you think. Makes you wonder."

"Evva will tell us," Bas says.

She's serene, with her pink-gold scales, leaning back against the front bulkhead of the mod. This one has no windows, though there's nothing to see. All they're doing is hurtling through space. A single set of emergency beacons flaring, but who knows if anything is nearby, who knows if anything ever will be. They could crash into an asteroid, a planet, and not know it until it happened.

This does not bug Sax in the slightest: If he's going to die an insulting death, he'd rather it be a surprise.

"Do you know that Dalachite thought the Oratus were the worst things in the galaxy?" Coorvin says of *Cobalt*'s now very-dead master, and now his white-tuft, black-furred face turned to look at them. "A failed experiment, it called you."

"Experiment?" Bas opens her eyes, yellow with black vertical slits. "What did it mean by that?"

"I don't know," Coorvin says. "It never elaborated. I didn't ask. Not my place, and not my interest."

"Which is?" Now Bas is as eager to carry the conversation as Sax was to start it.

"To find the answer, of course. The key to peace in the galaxy. That's the whole reason *Cobalt* was built. Why all of us signed up for the project."

"All of us?"

"Most left before you came," Coorvin said. "Took positions elsewhere as Dalachite changed its plans. As it became certain that the only way to survive was to eliminate everything else."

"It failed." Sax says.

"It came closer than you think," Coorvin counters.

But before that Flaum can continue, a buzzing noise breaks out inside the mod; the communications array sparking to life. Moments later a wet voice pours out amid static. High-pitched and drenched, like a river rushing through words.

"Hailing the mod, hailing the mod. Looks like you're going in the wrong direction. Care to tell us why? Seeing as we are here for *Cobalt* and *Cobalt* appears to be in a state of, can I say, disarray?"

The three of them meet each other's eyes. Then Coorvin jumps to respond.

"This is Coorvin, we evacuated the station. Critical power failure. Requesting pickup."

There's a burst of static and then the voice comes back. "Power failure! Well that's just downright bad. Guess we'll have to be keeping these supplies then. Maybe a delivery, sell them. Who did you say is in that mod, just you Coorvin?"

"A couple of others," Coorvin replies.

"We're closing in on your location, would like to know a bit more about those others if you wouldn't mind, Coorvin. You know how I dislike surprises."

Coorvin released the small button on the transponder. "Plake. She might kill us if I tell her what you are."

"Why would she?" Bas says. "We haven't done anything to her."

"You're Oratus. She's Vyphen."

That explains it. Sax rests his head back against the bulkhead. No Vyphen would willingly rescue an Oratus. It's hard to have much sympathy for the species that drove your own to ruin. That removed its sole reason for existence.

But then, the Vyphen didn't vanish. They discharged, streamed back into civilization, and found a new set of needs and wants. Did what other species had for cycles—found new desires that required certain means.

"She likes money, yes?" Sax hisses after a moment.

"She's a runner. Of course."

"Then tell her. Tell her we can pay her more than she'll know what to do with. Bas and I are respected. High up in the Vincere. They'll pay for our return."

The evac mod shakes. Something's docking with them. The transponder buzzes again.

"Coorvin, as you'll be able to tell unless that Amigga's stripped all your senses, we've docked with you. Going to open the door in a moment. Provided, of course, you tell me just why you're being so secretive. And, while you're at it, maybe explain to me why *Cobalt* decided to explode. Amigga generally don't let power failures take out their stations."

Coorvin looks at both Bas and Sax. The Oratus nod at the Flaum, who squeezes his eyes shut tight for a moment, then presses the transponder button.

"It's a pair of Oratus, Plake. I know what you're thinking. I know this isn't what you're hoping for, but they say they have money. They came in an official craft, on military business. They can pay you."

Just buzzing static. Then another thunk, a bang on the door.

"I see why you were trying to hide that fact from me, Coorvin. I really do. You think that I'm going to let two monsters onto my ship? You really think so?"

Sax reaches across Coorvin, presses a claw on the button. "Captain Plake, this is Sax, of the Vincere, third letter rank. I've never done anything to hurt the Vyphen. Never done anything to hurt you, your ship or your crew. My pair and I are only requesting transport to the closest station, and will pay you well for it. If you like, we can stay in your cargo hold. Out of your way. You'll collect a good sum for our delivery."

Sax releases the button, turns back to Bas, as he can here her amused hissing laugh.

"Never knew you could be so diplomatic," Bas replies.

"When I have to."

"Interesting," Plake's burbling bursts from the communications array. "I suppose I could bury my hatred for you for a little while. We're not too far from another station now, a place where you should be able to secure passage back to where you need to be. But when I open the door, it's my ship and my rules. You'll follow them, or I won't hesitate to melt you into slag. Nothing would make me happier."

"She sounds like a fighter," Sax says.

"She's efficient, and very protective of her ship." Coorvin replies.

There's a whistling noise of pressurizing air, and suddenly the outer locked door twists and shunts out away from the mod. Reveals a trio of creatures, all of them holding miners, and all of them pointing right at Sax and Bas.

"Coorvin, out you come," a pitch night-furred Flaum, with a small miner in one hand, beckons for Coorvin.

Coorvin doesn't wait either, scrambling out of the mod. Sax is slightly insulted, but it's not like the Flaum owes either Oratus anything. It's because of them he's no longer on the station, even if that means Coorvin's outside Dalachite's clutches.

"You two," hums a deep red Whelk, a slug-like beast that stands two meters tall, though its short, stubbly arms are no match for Sax's claws.

It holds a large weapon, no, Sax sees now: the miner is meshed into the sides of the Whelk's body. It's not the only modification showing on the slug; some sort of strange helmet with a cybernetic eyepiece rests on the Whelk's domed head. The Whelk's skin, a sliming crimson, shimmers as Sax looks at it.

Whatever they're dealing with here, this isn't an ordinary merchant ship.

"Time to come out, and you're gonna do it slow. As I say." The Whelk's voice comes from a slit it breaks in its skin, and the smattering of sounds come from undulations deep within its body. It's a strange noise, but it works. "First the pink one. Slow and easy."

Sax wants to protest. To argue and demand that he go before his pair, the better to let Bas know if they're going to be facing a surprise execution. Yet, the last thing he wants to do is antagonize their would be rescuers, so Sax stays quiet as Bas climbs over him. Her tail, ever so briefly, wraps around his own and gives a slight squeeze. Then she's gone, out through the circle and beyond the red Whelk. Sax sees the other Flaum peel away, the black-furred creature already chittering at Bas.

"Now you. You were the one that talked, right? The one that said cash for delivery?" The Whelk sounds smug as it says this.

Sax feels his claws clench. Forces them back open. Keeps his arms low. "I meant it. Deliver us, and your captain will get her money."

"How much you think she'll get for one instead of two? Or dead instead of alive?"

"You'll get one shot," Sax hisses, leaving his mouth open so the Whelk can see just how many teeth are waiting to bite. "You'll get one shot, and then I'll tear you in half. Then I'll tear the rest of your crew to pieces. I'll find your captain and I'll stuff her back in here with what's left of you, and shoot her into space. One shot. Better kill me or all of you are dead."

The skin beneath the Whelk's helmet changes, a streak of pale blue forming against the crimson in the shape of a nasty grin. "Glad we got the threats out of the way. At least I know you're actually Oratus. No Sevora come would bother with a speech like that. Come on, get out of there. The captain might hate you, but I know what you do. As one warrior to another, respect."

Sax follows the Whelk's lead, clambers out the evac mod and into a wide cargo bay. He notices first that this isn't some small shuttle, this is a serious ship. A freighter of size, and one that's currently hauling a ton of what looks like foodstuffs. The crates tower around them, with the broad doors for unloading closed to his left. Beneath him, Sax can feel the engines hum, the vibrations of the ionized gas pushing the ship forward. No doubt they'd be leaping soon.

Beyond the crates, the ceiling of the freighter begins to slope down and then spreads into three separate portals leaving straight, left and right.

"Don't think you'll be getting the grand tour though," the Whelk says as Sax looks around. "Captain Plake wants you restricted to the right module. Luckily, it's a good one. Kitchen, entertainment. Plenty of space for your big bodies."

"Thanks," Sax says.

"Don't thank me. Thank her."

The Whelk points with its fixed cannon by Sax, over the top of the crates to the straight-away portal, which had just opened to reveal a feathered, smooth-skinned yellowish creature, with two long legs, and a pair of feathered arms that extend to circular, webbed hands with nubby fingers. Large round eyes, rising up over the top of her head, rotate towards Sax. Her mouth opens, and Sax can see, even from this distance, the folded curl of her tongue.

"Agra-Red," Plake announces, her voice just as gurgling as it sounded through the transponder. "Get them locked away. I want to leap out of this dismal patch of space and kick these two off my ship before I decide to kill them."

"Plake's a wonder, isn't she?" Agra-Red, the Whelk, laughs and nudges Sax forward with the edge of his miner.

Delightful.

Vimelia.

Ignos sends me the name as the shuttle passes into a large cavern beneath the ground. I can't even see the end of it, as the moment we leave the tunnel, a light, bright and white, opens above us and tracks the shuttle, sliding just ahead and guiding us towards an empty space. It's a blinding shine, and the light washes out anything outside that I could see. The engines slow down and stop as the shuttle lowers itself to the ground. Struts extend and the whole thing settles with the slightest of bumps.

Vimelia is my home.

"Does this mean we can get out now?" Viera says, and I see that her netting is gone.

The straps holding Viera's feet to the ground retract and in a second mine do as well. A short, quick snap, and then I stumble forward, suddenly free. My legs are stiff, my knees hurt, but I can move.

The Sevora did not begin here, but this is where we have gone. Where we live.

I catch myself on the terminals, the screens that used to show a map of the galaxy, now dead and blank. I don't understand. This shuttle belonged to the Oratus. To Sax and Bas. Why did it come here?

Because you told it to. Once it arrived, my friends guided it down. Do not be afraid, Kaishi.

"Do you know where we are?" Malo asks me, and as he says the words, he puts his hand on my shoulder.

That's the first touch I've had since we left. Since I learned that I took my two friends to place so far from home that it doesn't even exist in our imaginations. I almost break right then. Almost collapse at the idea that we've come so far and yet are nowhere near where we need to go.

Tell them.

"This is where Ignos, where its kind live," I say, though I can't quite bring myself to turn and look at Malo and Viera as I talk. "When it told me what numbers to press, it sent the shuttle here."

"The creature tricked us," Viera says. "Seems like we ought to get it out of your head and underneath my boot."

"For once, I agree with the Lunare." Malo's voice is angry, resigned. "It's betrayed you, Kaishi. We can't trust it anymore."

"We didn't have a choice," I say. "We don't know how to fly this thing. We didn't know where to go—"

I want to keep going, to pour out my frustrations one after another, when a whooshing sound from behind us, towards the middle of the shuttle, draws me away. Closes my mouth. Viera and Malo don't hesitate though. The Lunare steps back, near me, and puts her clenched fists up near her face. Malo does his own version, settling into a crouch and keeping his eyes straight ahead.

I see it then. Something that looks much the same as what we left behind. Only instead of gray or pink gold, these scales are a strange faded yellow, and many have black around the edges, a few are even missing. The Oratus still stands tall, and it's flanked by a pair of very real, non-fuzzy Flaum that stomp into the shuttle behind it. Whereas Sax and Bas didn't seem to wear any clothing, this one sports strange black metal pieces. Bracelets around its wrists and ankles. When it looks at me, with burning green eyes, I get the sense that it sees possibility.

"Please, put yourselves at rest," the Oratus says. "I am Nasiya, leader of the Sevora. Which one of you is the master?"

"I am," I say, stepping in front of Viera and Malo.

No sense having them take the blame, get hurt if there's an attack.

"You entered the code to come here?" Nasiya replies in the harsh hissing voice Oratus have.

"Ignos told me what to enter," I reply.

This only seems to confuse the creature, and his eyes narrow.

"Told you?" The Oratus doesn't turn around, but I can tell he's not speaking to me when he says, "We confirmed that there are no weapons on the ship, yes?"

"Of course," a brown-furred Flaum replies. "The scan showed that even though this is a Vincere ship, there is at least one hosted creature among these."

The Oratus centers his eyes on me again. "One hosted creature. I see three. Though, much to my chagrin, I know not what you are."

Answer him.

I don't know what to say. Part of me doesn't want to say anything. Wants to push back, demand that we be taken home. Part of me wants to fight, to resist. But we've been fighting for so long. It feels like an eternity since we left the city, Damantum, on the march to stop the Oratus invaders. In truth, I don't know how long it's been.

I do know that I'm tired. My head hurts and my bones are weak. I need food, sleep. And the last thing I can do right now is struggle.

"We are humans," I say. "From a planet called Earth. Ignos came to me, and lives inside me now."

Things happen quickly. Nasiya triggers some invisible signal. His shape, those pale yellow scales, fuzz and then vanish entirely. I barely process this before the two Flaum beckon us forward and push the three of us out of the shuttle.

As we go down the ramp, I see a dozen slug-like creatures standing off to the right holding what Ignos calls instruments. They sweep up the ramp after we leave it, and sounds of ripping metal, shifting crates, and loud yells pour back to us.

Now that I'm in the bay, I get a better view of the giant space and notice it's packed with other ships, some coming and going, those lights popping up to guide them. The Flaum lead us through the dark, though I'm not sure how the Sevora hosts can see where they're going, until I start stepping along the ground. Low green circles appear—it seems the ground itself changes color—directing me where to go.

It reads me, Kaishi. Vimelia connects to me the way I connect to you.

The three of us follow the Flaum, with more walking behind. If they carry some form of weapon, I can't see it, and once the threat of our execution dies away and my pounding heart slows, I actually start looking around. We pass from the large cavern into beautiful hall-ways. Or at least, they appear that way to me. The walls are coded in waves of shifting color that change as we pass by. A section may start as swaths of bright blue and morph with a wave of green that fades into pink and yellow as we leave it behind. I ask Ignos what it means.

Just as you have your paintings, the Sevora have ours. Much of our history is told through patterns of light and how they change. It is a language, it is a story. One I will tell you someday if you like.

The hallway ends in a long chamber with a wall full of circular doors. Lines of species stand in front of them, stepping in through those openings as others step out. We go to the largest one, on the far right. It's the only one without a line, and also the only one with a red line around the doorway. In between each of the circles, screens display messages warning of closures, delays, and news full of terms I don't understand.

"When it opens," the lead Flaum announces in its squeaky voice. "The three of you will move in first. You will take your seats on the far side as best you are able. We will follow, and when we are secured, we will proceed."

As if waiting for its speech to end, as soon as the Flaum quiets, the circular doorway shunts open and reveals a strange pearl disk waiting for us. The three Flaum in front of me part, and wave us through.

"Guess we're riding this thing?" Viera asks.

"I suppose?" I say. "I don't think we have a choice."

"You mean we're prisoners again?" Viera replies, and I can't help smiling at her sarcasm.

Humor is like a cup full of cold water right now; refreshing and vital.

"We will do what we've done before," Malo says, and I notice he's switched to the Charre tongue.

It works here, as it did on *Cobalt*. The Flaum escorting us stare around at each other, confused. They don't know what Malo said. We have our secret, and I shake my head slightly to warn them not to use it. Not here.

I lead the way, walk through the circle door—warning Malo to watch his head—and step onto the white disk. Around us is a cerulean-shaded transparent tube. Every so often black lines mark the seams between pieces, the seals holding it together. I can see ahead of me that the tube curls up and slightly to the right. Away from the bay.

I'm about to ask where the seats are when the disk shivers and, seeming to arise from nothing, three individual chairs mold up out of the surface. They're barely wide enough to fit me, and Viera and Malo squeeze into theirs, all of us arrayed in the line, at odd angles. As soon as we sit down, like the straps on the shuttle, more pearly stuff leaks up from the floor and wraps itself around our arms and legs. Three Flaum get in behind us, and this time I see that the chairs are indeed flowing up from the disk, making the platform itself shrink in the process. Amorphous material, forming itself to the needs of the riders.

"While we are en route, try not to speak," the lead Flaum warns us, though he doesn't explain why.

There's no signal, no sign. One moment we're sitting on the platform in our cramped chairs and the next we're shooting up through the tube. Rising upward at a velocity I've never felt before. Far faster than dashing through the trees. Wind blows my hair forward, dark strands slashing across my face. I close my eyes.

No. Keep them open. Look.

I do, then. And I'm glad. What I see around me is beyond anything I've seen before. From the shuttle, up above, the city seemed false somehow. Unreal. I couldn't reach out and touch it, I wasn't level with the buildings and the swirling, swooping structures. But here, as the tube rockets us out of the cavern and into the day, I'm stunned at built beauty rivaling the jungle flowers of my home.

Glittering structures of all heights and all colors rise up around us. Some resemble shapes I've seen on Earth: squares, or tall towers. Others rise as triangles or sloping domes. Thin spires that lead to cubes raised high in the air.

Next to us, on either side, other tubes rise up and glide in parallel, then cut away or up or down. New ones join our track. We shift, though I don't really feel it aside from a slight jolt in the scenery. All I know is that we're moving. Going somewhere.

The Flaum in front of us don't seem to react. Their eyes pin to me, Malo and Viera. They're so serious. I don't know why, seeing as we're surrounded by marvels.

In Solare legends, we talk of the great cities of the gods; gold and silver and jade everywhere. Whole palaces built of gems that sparkled with an infinite shine. If I could have chosen a place that described those tales, Vimelia would be it.

The Sevora cannot choose the qualities of the species we take, but we can choose what we create. Express ourselves through the worlds we make. What we wish we would see around us. Vimelia is a representation of what we wish to be.

Beyond the buildings I see a tan sky cluttered with moving specks and shifting forms. All shapes, from the angular angry things that escorted us in, to larger floating barges drifting through the air. Others rocket up from the surface, screeching towards the sky before vanishing. There's so much motion everywhere that it almost makes me dizzy. The jungle, aside from buzzing insects, was often still.

I try to take a breath, to ask Viera and Malo what they think, what they see, but when I push air out of my lungs it doesn't want to go. The words emerge and die instantly. Squeaks amid the constant roar of wind. That's why they warned us not to speak.

The platform twists and swirls through a series of interlocking gates and I sense a sudden fall, though I don't see it, and we slow to a crawl as we pass beneath a series of large, metal loops. The sky vanishes for a long moment and we're plunged into dark.

A switch station.

Then we are out again, this time moving in a straighter line. I can see the switch station behind us, and from the outside, it looks like the Amigga; so many tubes looping in from everywhere. Platforms shoot in from all angles and sides and then back out again in different directions.

We're nearly there. You should know, Nasiya and the others want to help you. Help us. You have to trust them.

Ignos ruins the magic of the moment by bringing back reality. How can I trust them? How can I trust any of these things?

Because you have no choice. Because you are far from home and the only way back rests in us giving it to you, Kaishi. You are not an Empress, you're not a young girl with the protection of her tribe or her father. You are alone and you are in danger. So let us help you.

I don't respond. Not directly, anyway. Ignos can read my emotions, scan my thoughts. I can't hide anything from the creature, but at least I can ignore its responses. So I do, and I watch the movement until the platform begins to slow. Until the sky goes dark and we move under a white awning. Then our ride comes to a rest. Once the Flaum rise, their seats once more flow back into the platform. Like a melting candle.

The three creatures move to the circular door, which shifts open as they approach. Two more of the slug-like things on the other side, bright green in color and holding miners of their own.

"We don't need more escorts," the lead Flaum says, loud enough for me to hear.

"There's been an alert," one of the slugs says, its voice a staccato hum. "Clarity's Dawn. Nasiya wants these three protected. Heavily."

Clarity's Dawn? I don't know what that means.

It's not for you to worry about.

"That was about the craziest thing I've ever seen," Viera says as we stand up. I almost fall as the chair vanishes beneath me, but Malo catches my arm and holds me steady.

"It's amazing," I say. "Did you see all of those things flying through the air? We could do that someday. Back home."

"You two, stop talking," the lead Flaum growls, turning back to us. "Follow, please. And stay silent. There'll be time enough for talking later."

"No need to get snappy," Viera murmurs, but the Flaum doesn't hear her.

We follow them, out away from the tube onto another landing. This one isn't as crowded, but whereas the species in the cavern came in all types and clothes, from rags to armor to metal and further, these all seem to sport the same greenish orange clothing. Many of them, whether on fur, smooth skin or something else entirely, wear a simple square badge with an orange circle overlaid on a pale green surface.

The symbol of my people. The orange is us, a strong line against outsiders. Protecting the life contained within.

Beyond the loading area, we walk into a tall, wide hall with sloping sides reaching up to a vaulted roof. I'm reminded of the Vaos, the grand temple in Damantum, though in its material and design this Sevora building is nothing like it. Rather, I feel the same grandeur, a pulse of power resonating here, just as it does back home.

As we walk, I feel the eyes of a thousand things watching me. Some friendly, curious. Others angry or threatened.

"Do you think we're wanted?" I ask. "Some of these are looking at us like we're enemies."

"I sure hope so, seeing as they took us here. Seeing as it's your buddy that put the code into the shuttle." Viera's scanning the crowds, and I see her hands drift towards her belt, though there's no weapon there.

"She didn't have a choice, Viera. None of us did. None of us do."

Malo, always defending me. Even when I don't deserve it.

At my friend's words, the Flaum leader jerks his head back towards us and snaps his furry fingers. His point made, Malo quiets and I say nothing. Instead we watch and walk through one mesmerizing room after another until at last we find ourselves at what appears to be the top.

It's an enclosed room, with clear see-through walls all around. The floor appears made entirely of the same white stuff as the platform we rode. The Flaum direct us to the middle of the room where, as we stand, a table rises. Only this isn't a rectangle or square, it's a circle forming around us. Trapping us inside. Small chairs grow beneath us, forcing us to sit.

The Flaum back away towards the door we came in, and then leave entirely.

"I think I could jump over this," Viera says.

"There must be a reason we're here," I say. "So don't do anything stupid."

"She's talking to you, Viera," Malo says.

"I'm talking to all of us, myself included."

There's a flicker. The fuzziness, and then again the pale yellow Oratus appears near the back window. It stares at the three of us for a moment, passing its gaze from one of us to the next.

"Welcome to Vimelia. Welcome to your new home."

There's silence for a moment, and then Viera says what we're all thinking, "Home? This isn't our home."

Nasiya looks at my friend. Spreads its teeth in a grin. "You are unhosted, yes?"

"If you mean that I don't have one of those slug things in my head like Kaishi here, yeah. I'm unhosted."

"Then you've yet to understand. You will see soon enough that

Vimelia is yours. All of you will. I'm very excited that you've come. Very excited that you've decided to join us."

"We decided nothing," I say. "We were tricked. We didn't want to come here."

"Fortune sometimes happens upon those who don't expect it." Nasiya throws away my remark. "In a moment, your meals will arrive. Then, you'll be shown your quarters. Tomorrow, your true tour of Vimelia will begin."

We don't get a chance to ask it questions; Nasiya fuzzes out and vanishes, leaves us in the white room alone.

Nasiya has never been much for words. He prefers action, as you will see.

I shake my head. I don't care about Nasiya. What I do care about, though, is getting off this planet. Getting back home.

But even those concerns fall away when the door behind whisks open and the Flaum walk back in, our guards followed by other Flaum wielding trays instead of weapons. Sitting on the silver serving platters is stuff I recognize from *Cobalt*. The same strange pastes Bas served me on that cold metal station.

As the Flaum come into the room, the table and chairs surrounding us melt down to the floor. New ones rise up, more adequately spaced for a meal. A large, flat saucer surface, with rounded stumps for chairs whose tops are just large enough for us to sit on. When we don't make an immediate move, the lead Flaum, the black-furred one that's been leading us the entire way, waves with his rifle towards the setup.

It's not difficult to interpret what they want.

As we sit, the other Flaum place the trays of paste in front of each of us. Then brown bowls with blue specks are set next to those, filled with a clear liquid. It looks like water, but none of us touch it until one of the serving Flaums pantomimes a drinking motion.

"Think it's poisoned?" Viera says, in our secret Charre tongue, as we pick up the bowls.

"They have easier ways to kill us," Malo replies, then takes a long drink.

We both watch. He might choke and collapse. Turn purple. Or, for all I know, sprout fur and morph into a Flaum.

Ridiculous. It's just water.

As if I trust Ignos now. But after a few breaths, and Malo taking a second drink, I decide to follow. My throat's been dry and scratchy for a long time—we didn't exactly get many breaks on *Cobalt*—and the cool water feels delicious and silky on my throat. Heavier than the rivers back home.

Vimelia's water comes from deep beneath its surface. What you taste is the planet's own flavor.

"How do you know what we can drink and eat?" Viera asks after her own sip. "Or does everyone run on water and roast pork?"

"This room," says the lead Flaum. "Scans what you are. The flakes of your skin, the breath you exhale, the heat from your bodies. We form a chemical composite, an estimation of what you require to survive, and provide our best guess."

"Guess? So there's a chance you could kill us?"

"There are always risks with new species," the Flaum's chitter gets low. "Usually it takes a few accidents to get a perfect calibration."

"I'll try to help—you have any actual meat here?" Viera pokes at the nutrient goop with her finger. The yellow slime shivers at her touch.

"Meat?" The Flaum looks back at Viera. "Only an uncivilized worm would eat raw animal proteins."

"You calling me a worm?"

Before the Flaum can clarify, a black square on its belt shifts to a bright green color and emits a single, bright chime. Without another word, it and the other Flaum turn and leave us alone in the room. The door shuts behind them, and we're alone.

I try a taste of a blue-green ball on the tray. It's mostly flavorless, a hint of mint, yet I feel what I'm eating is incredibly healthy. My stomach thrills as I swallow the bites. Yet I don't like the texture, the lack of nature in the ball. It's not from home.

But you live. Which is, after all, the most important thing.

Viera and Malo struggle like me, with hunger's desire pushing us through the motions. We use our hands; shovel the stuff into our mouths. I'm not surprised we didn't get any tools. Things that could be used as weapons.

"Tastes like dirt," Viera says.

"I agree," Malo replies. "I'd hoped we had seen the last of this on the station."

"I'd eat anything from home again," I say. "Even those peppers you gave me seem like miracles."

I smile at the memory and where it leads; the idea that, someday, I'd be eating another fish tortilla, spreading those peppers on the white soft meat and taking a slow bite. Feel that heat rushing up and down my throat.

Truly, it's only when you leave home that you appreciate it fully. Yet you will find plenty to like here. Give it time.

We barely clear the trays before the Flaum come back in. This time there's no talk as they wave us up, and the lead Flaum ignores questions about where we're going. Directs us back to the tubes. There we board another platform, which takes us on a whizzing journey through the city. The skies have turned from bright beige to a soft orange, and I can make out a glowing, large orb on the far horizon that stretches like a mountain.

This is as low as our star will go. We have a strange orbit here, and no true night unless you go beneath the surface.

The heat of a jungle day flashes through my mind at the thought of endless light and I don't understand how Vimelia isn't melting?

Because of what we sprinkled throughout the atmosphere. Reflective dust gathers and pushes back the light and heat. Carefully controlled. Before that, all you see lived underground. In the cool dark.

The platform stops at a long and tall building that looks like sculpted emerald. I wonder why for second until I remember the badges. The life.

Yes. These are the quarters where you will stay until you join us.

I don't want to know what that means. We follow the Flaum off the platform and through a short tour into a long and wide chamber. On either side, going up many stories, are long walkways with doors, ones with the metal bars, and no curtains.

"This is a prison," Viera says.

"We don't know that," I reply.

"Even if it is, we don't have a choice." Malo kills the conversation.

The Flaum take us up a twisting stair to the third level and then out onto a landing. From here I can make out that many of the cells are occupied. Behind the bars, shapes lurk, and some press their faces, their snouts, their eyed tentacles towards us.

More Flaum stalk the walkways looking back at their charges. Two or three on each level striding back and forth. Some carrying food or other things they pass through the bars to the intended recipient. It's like a small city, although it's clear there's one thing not on offer here; freedom.

You'll get that when your friends are hosted, when you agree to help us.

We reach three cells in a line. They're empty, and the only thing inside is the same white floor as anywhere else.

The lead Flaum taps his right claw on the side of the gate. When I realize what's happening, I try to count out the sequence but it's too long, too fast. The bars rise towards the ceiling, and then another Flaum pushes me in. The bars come down, and then the other Flaum push Malo and Viera on to the next one.

As they walk away, Malo throws me a worried look and I try to reply with confidence I'm not feeling. I tell myself there's nothing we can do here now anyway, best to go along. Best to wait for another chance.

"This cell is tuning to you," the lead Flaum says to me through the bars. As he finishes the words, the white floor flashes blue for a moment before settling back into its pearly color. "It's designed to make furniture. Think of what you want, and it will give you what you need. It will not give you weapons, tools or other means of escape. I recommend sleep, if your species needs it."

The Flaum turns and walks away, leaving me alone in the cell.

Go ahead. Use it.

Following Ignos' instructions, I think of a bench, a simple chair there in the corner near the door. In a second something rises up and forms the wooden bamboo construct—though it stays the alabaster color—on the floor. It looks right for me. So I sit in it. Strong and solid. I imagine my small cot bed from my palace. It forms in the back corner, blankets even coming out of the stuff, although, when I press my hands to them, they feel more fake, artificial than what I'm used to. Not real wool.

When I put my hands on the bed, I remember the bracelet on my wrist. The Cache. Before Ignos can stop me, I open it and dip deep inside looking for answers.

And find many.

The crimson Whelk slithers its legless self in front of Sax through the bays. Leads Sax and Bas through the maze of cargo towards the front of the ship and the three different doorways pointing to seperate modules. Agra-Red seems happy to talk about the crew, the ship, and Sax is more than happy to let it. Pays to learn about your enemies.

"So you see this place, built courtesy of Plake herself. Took the ship as a prize when her captain retired and the others fought for it. None of'em are left." The note of pride in Agra-Red's voice isn't hard to catch. "From there, she built her crew in the usual way."

Agra-Red pauses, intentionally waiting for a question. So Bas asks one.

"And what's that?" Bas hisses.

"Go to the most worthless pilots you can find, hire them, wait till they rob you, and then go find the right ones," Agra-Red shakes its head as it says this, the lack of bones causing the motion to make the entire creature ripple. "I've been doing this a long time, and you wouldn't believe the number of sob stories I've heard from captains who feel they've been cheated somehow. You hire wrong, you'll get wronged."

This continues until they reach the front, and then Agra-Red gestures towards a ladder to the right, ascending out from the cargo module to the rest of the ship. Agra-Red, and Whelks in general, can't climb, so it settles into a small mold-colored platform. When Agra-Red gets on it, the platform rises faster than the Oratus can climb.

Speed is important on a ship when spare seconds fiddling with rungs could mean the difference between an explosive decompression or a stable repair.

"Since then, we've been running scrap, food supplies and more to everywhere we can find. Because, and I don't figure you Oratus know this, there's not much left to the galaxy these days except sending cargo."

"What do you mean?" Sax asks. "Most of the galaxy is safe. Most of it's inhabited."

"Inhabited by what?" Agra-Red replies. "Boring, normal people? Ones content to live on the dirt rather than scorch the sky? No. You Oratus took the war, took the meaning from my life. From all of ours. Now you have two choices. You hire on like me, run cargo and count your coins and wait for a better life. Or you get desperate, capture a bit of excitement playing pirate until your life catches up with you and you wind up slagged, floating above some planet forever."

"You take a grim view of the galaxy," Bas says.

"You know my name? Agra-Red?"

The Oratus nod.

"My home and my color. I'm still around, but Agra itself? Bombed into nothing. The Sevora established a foothold and now it's just gone. Haven't found a single one of my friends or my family that survived. Would you be happy tilling dirt or tending a bar if that happened to your home?" When Sax and Bas don't have a reply, Agra-Red laughs, a sick thing with more than its share of ruefulness in it. "Ah, I forget. You monsters don't have homes."

Sax could correct the Whelk, but doesn't. It wouldn't matter anyway.

Agra-Red leads them through a short hallway which opens into a broad, spectacularly filthy kitchen. Stuff, like half-eaten nutrient packs, crates, bags and bits and pieces of paper and other trash lay about everywhere, with a thin cylinder in the center of it all, as though someone's been trying and failing to toss the garbage inside it.

"Welcome to your space," Agra-Red says. "Oh yeah, that there's Engee. She makes these messes."

Sax doesn't see what Agra-Red is pointing at until it moves. Sax thinks the cylinder is a waste bin, but now he sees it's a Teven, only instead of the usual sandy-colored shell, this one is metallic. Black and silver. With a bunch of things he mistakes for trash hanging off the shell's various holes.

"I'm being kicked out?" Engee exclaims, the sounds coming hollow through the holes, like a whistle. "But I'm in the middle of something."

"Not anymore," Agra-Red says. "We picked up refugees. They need a place to stay. And it's yours."

"Plake gave them this?"

"Captain's orders. Get out of here."

"At least you could be nice about it," Engee replies, and then the trash can moves. Waddles close to Sax. He can't make out the Teven itself inside, at least until a small arm shoots out from one of the holes into one of the tools hanging off the side and lifts it up. Sax notices the hanging things aren't just garbage, but are some sort of attachment. The Teven sticks it towards them and Sax sees a strange red eye, one that quickly flashes green. "They're not hosted. No Sevora in either of them."

"That's too bad. Here I thought I was gonna have myself a couple roasted Oratus." Agra-Red deadpans.

"You're expecting us to stay in all this garbage?" Bas says to the Whelk.

"Not my problem," Agra-Red replies. "Plake says we're leaping soon so if you want a comfortable ride, I'd find a seat."

Agra-Red and Engee head out of the room, slapping a wall panel on the way that shunts closed a door. The two Oratus are alone, stuck in a disaster area. Sax sweeps his eyes over the mess. Buried under some mounds of wrapping looks like some old crash chairs. Things that could be used, if needed, to ride out a leap.

"I wonder where Coorvin went," Bas says as she starts picking through the junk.

Most of it looks like scrap metal; parts torn off of other things collected here in a giant jumble. Some are set aside, on top of the table the Teven was sitting at when they came in. The beginnings of a project, something long and cylindrical. A weapon, or maybe an engine. Sax isn't much for gadgets unless he's using them.

"That Flaum took him," Sax replies. "Coorvin seems to know them."

Bas rakes her tail, sweeps the jumble from the table and moves the clutter onto the floor. It falls fast, which tells Sax that the ship is using magnetic gravity. An electrical charge run through magnets in the base of the ship. Keeps things tugged towards the center. Doesn't work so well on living creatures, but then, Sax and Bas are used to keeping themselves stable in unstable places.

"How long do you think Coorvin lived with the Amigga?" Bas hisses as she and Sax clear junk away from their seats.

There's a net across the back of the wide chairs, and they each pull it on. Slip their claws through the gaps and watch the stars spin from the small viewscreen on the wall.

"Long enough to go insane, I think," Sax says. "Or nearly. He doesn't smell normal."

Which, for Flaum, meant fear. Skittishness. Sweat and shedding fur. At least when Oratus come around.

"How should we get back to Evva?" Bas asks.

"We could take this ship if we wanted to," Sax replies. "Except I haven't seen evidence of a crime. We would need to declare it a military necessity. Or get them to do something criminal."

"That shouldn't be too hard."

"Then we confiscate it, fly this ship wherever we need to go."

"Where is that?" Bas says. "To the center? Right to the Chorus and the main Vincere fleet?"

The question catches Sax by surprise. Why wouldn't they head back to the Vincere? Why wouldn't they rejoin the war against the Sevora?

"Are you suggesting there's elsewhere we should go?"

"We just killed an Amigga, Sax," Bas replies. "Yes, it was self-defense, but the Chorus doesn't look favorably on those that kill its own. Going back might just put us in a cell."

Sax waits. It's not like Bas to start a perfectly logical explanation without following it up with something more interesting. Besides, self-defense would play well. A deranged Amigga, left alone on the edge of the galaxy, gone insane with its own experiments, tried to kill both Sax, Bas, and three specimens that could mean an end to the bloodiest conflict in recorded history?

Sax feels he has an argument.

"But most importantly" Bas finishes. "I don't think Evva is there."

Sax is about to ask why, when Plake's voice booms over the ship's intercom. An announcement, a call to say that the ship is about to leap and they should all get ready for it. From there it's a quick count-down. Sax takes deep breaths with his vents. It's weird not being on the bridge, weird being surrounded by all this random garbage as the universe tilts sideways and he spins through the cascade of sensations that come with the leap. That come with the tearing and repairing of his atomic structure.

At least it's quick. Mere moments and then Sax blinks from one part of the galaxy to another. It's a physical cost, and a mental one, but thus far Sax hasn't had any lasting effects and he's done hundreds of the things. So long as you know where you're going, leaping isn't that bad.

In seconds both Oratus are out of their webbing. A few more after that and they're both standing by the door. Waiting.

"Don't know whether you're getting any ideas," Plake's voice comes over the intercom. "We're not letting you out of there until we're docked. I don't like randoms running around my ship in the best of times, and these aren't those. Sit tight. We're coming in on *Scrapper Station*, and once we get there you can get off and leave me alone."

"So much hate for the species protecting your lives," Sax growls, though he doesn't think the intercom is sending anything back to the captain.

"It's not hate, Sax. It's caution." Bas says. "*Scrapper Station* isn't a civilized place. We're not going here because she wants to turn us over to the Vincere."

The Whelk, Agra-Red, is right about one thing—when the Oratus imposed their version of order on the Vincere, they displaced the ragged cluster of species who'd made generations out of serving the grand vision of those twelve Amiggas making up the Chorus. Cast out and uncared for, the sudden influx of pilots, mechanics, soldiers and support staff began forging their own destinies in a galaxy that, so long as they weren't being too violent, didn't spare a thought for them.

Sax hasn't been to many of these outposts—the ones he's visited are those that fell to Sevora incursions, and he left most of those drifting ruins—and he's not thrilled to visit another. The dirty room they're in now serves as an accurate impression for what they'll encounter on *Scrapper Station*; trash, both of the physical and mental variety.

"If the Vyphen betrays us, then we'll make sure she regrets it," Sax says, taking up position just outside the door and looking back to Bas, who seems content to lounge in her chair.

"Murder doesn't go unpunished, Sax."

The words twist Sax for a moment. He's been a sanctioned killer for the entirety of his existence, given permission to do whatever is necessary to advance the Vincere's, the Chorus', agenda. The species on this ship, on the station, aren't Sevora. Aren't enemy agents. Unless Sax feels his own life is threatened, he doesn't have any standing to slaughter Plake and her crew.

"I don't like this anymore," Sax sighs through his vents.

"You'll recall I suggested killing the humans back when we left Earth," Bas replies. "We could have left them to Dalachite, departed *Cobalt* and we wouldn't be here now."

"That perversion deserved its end."

The ship shudders as it begins its docking phase. The magnetic gravity decreases to prevent interference with *Scrapper Station*'s own systems, and Bas, with a flick of her tail, sends a pile of gray-metal tiles floating through the air.

"We'll find a way to contact Evva from the station," Bas says, her eyes tracking the chips. "She'll know how to get us back home."

The two of them share the space for a while longer, feeling every part of the docking process in the freighter's shakes. It takes far longer to dock a ship of this size than it does the shuttle Sax and Bas used to fly—the freighter's too large to simply fit in a bay. Instead, *Scrapper Station* uses a series of arms to 'catch' the ship, once the freighter matches the station's velocity, and then it extends a long tube to the passenger airlock.

When that tube connects, the door to the Oratus' room shunts open, and for the first time Sax is face-to-face with Plake. The Vyphen is half Sax's height, and her red skin shimmers beneath the thick white and yellow feathers running along her back and arms. In low gravity, and on the small world the Vyphens called home, Plake could fly.

Not that it would help her escape Sax's claws in tight quarters like these. By her eyes, narrowed and deep green, Plake knows this. But she doesn't crouch away, flinch, or clench her webbed hands when Sax glares down at her.

Plake has the respect of her crew, and Sax begins to see why.

Agra-Red and one of the black-furred Flaum stand behind Plake, both with miners trained on the Oratus. Backing up their commander's courage with the firepower it deserves.

"You'll follow me," Plake says. "They'll follow you. Let's go."

As they leave the room, Sax hears the churning, banging, shifting noise of unloading cargo. He throws a look over the railing and back down the deep bay. Bright white lights pierce the soft yellow of the freighter's illumination, showing where the robo-skiffs are working. Grabbing crates with their magnet arms, floating with them to the bay's cargo airlock, where, after pressure's drained, the skiffs would take their goodies across a short expanse to the station.

"I thought those were meant for *Cobalt*," Sax says to Plake's back as they move.

"*Cobalt* doesn't exist anymore," Plake replies without turning her head. "Figure that makes them mine to sell."

"Does the Chorus agree?"

"Who's going to tell them? You?"

Sax bares his teeth, though the Vyphen can't see it. He doesn't need Bas' tail tap to keep his mouth shut this time.

The connection tube doesn't give them much more than a view, through thick glass, of the station. It's enough to tell Sax why *Scrapper Station* has its name—built in the aftermath of a thick Vincere-Sevora battle, *Scrapper Station* looks like someone swept up a bunch of junk and glued it all together. There's no semblance of organization, no planning—the station shoots out in all directions, with jutting points and nodes veering out into space.

There's no planet near here, which means no gravity grabbing all these lanky parts. Only asteroids, stocked with valuable metals and the reason for the fight in the first place. As they walk, Sax can see small mining ships blasting to and from tiny bays, grabbing platinum and gold from spinning rocks and returning it. A big refiner craft, like Plake's freighter, is doing its own docking procedure. It's shaped like a cylinder, and the raw ore will be loaded into one end, refined during the trip, and the cleaned product will be ready on delivery to whatever crafters want it.

"There's more here than I expected," Bas says.

"None of you know what's going on in the galaxy you're trying to protect," Plake replies. "You see all those little guys? Grabbing the metals? They're supplying you with all your weapons. One run at a time."

"Would you rather we focused on this station than the Sevora?" Sax cuts in. "We're keeping you alive."

"By destroying *Cobalt*? Didn't think it was the enemy."

Sax doesn't have an answer for that. It would be easy to say Dalachite tried to kill them, that it was performing strange, reprehensible experiments, but the galaxy depends on its hierarchy and the Amigga stand at the top. Undermining their authority goes against everything Sax, and those who fight in the Vincere, stand for.

So he marches in silence until they're through the tube, passing through a dented door—evidence, perhaps, of a few desperate entry attempts—and into one of *Scrapper Station*'s arrival areas.

Rather than the cluster of species mingling their way back and forth, dealing in promises both physical and not, the wide room stands deserted except for a trio. Two of them, crag-like Lutos, hold large miners in their black-dirt arms. The single-eyed, mud-coated monsters don't talk much, and Sax is surprised to see any of them outside of their molten puddle of a home planet.

"Just as you promised, Plake," the voice comes from the third, the only species capable of talking, a yellow mound with a pair of stalked, bulbous eyes. "I'll take them."

The Ooblot says the words. Sax is ready to dodge, but the fire doesn't come from in front, from the Lutos. No, the searing pain, the numbing shock that sends the Oratus down into black strikes from behind.

The Cache spills Vimelia's past out to me, and I'm surprised at how similar it is to our own. Ignos gave the impression that its people were ordered, were *above* us humans, but they fight and struggle as much as we do, even if they've exchanged spears for words and lifetimes sentenced to darkness for our sacrifices atop our Tiers.

I find out, too, that they're losing.

The slaughter of the Sevora at the hands of the Vincere and their Oratus—I remember Sax and Bas and wouldn't want to be the target of their deadly claws, much less an army of them—is a saga that seems to go on forever. I wind up turning away from the Cache's litany of battles playing out in my mind for fear of being lost among the swirling ships exploding into mini novas.

The shift brings me to the Chorus, and the Cache begins to struggle; brushing up against the edges of its knowledge feels like grasping at a fading memory—there's tantalizing wisps of possibility, but nothing concrete. Nothing beyond the sure sense of more Amigga, and their power over everything.

And hate. Such a feeling of it that I get angry. I'm not *with* myself and yet my thundering heart races my lungs in a sprint towards exhaustion. These things, these terrible Amigga are the reason the galaxy is in so much pain, the reason for all the death, destruction, and war that's tearing species after species apart.

"Kaishi!"

It's not Ignos breaking apart the Cache's hold on me this time but an actual voice. One I recognize as the fog of relentless knowledge clears away.

"We have to go, Empress," I parse Malo's words now, and turn around, towards the bars.

What I see doesn't mesh with the reality I left behind. The lighting's all wrong, for one. I'd jumped into the Cache with a bronzed orange glow filtering through the top of the prison, but now it's a brighter white. Though that only serves as a backdrop for the characters looking in at me:

Malo and Viera star front and center, both looking mostly like I last saw them, though Malo's wearing a warning on his face, while Viera shakes her head and looks confused. Glancing past them, it's not hard to see why.

A bluish-green creature lurks between the two, hunched over and wearing something I can only call a cloak, though with the way it catches and turns the light, which makes the creature flicker, it's clearly more than anything my father wore to our ceremonies. In its hands are a pair of small miners, both angled ever-so-slightly towards Malo and Viera. Its swamp-green eyes, though, are locked on me. By the time its mouth opens, and the long, pink tongue inside it shivers, I'm already moving to what's going on behind.

Where are the guards?

Ignos echoes my own question, and I wonder if the constant flashes of blue and red behind my friends have anything to do with the conspicuous absence. The blasts come from down below and up above, accompanied by occasional shrieks of pain or howled words I don't understand.

"Kaishi. Focus." Malo's command yanks me back.

"I'm here." I move towards the bars, though they're still closed.

I'm still trapped.

Don't. They mean to destroy you. Ruin any chance you have of peace.

Which doesn't mean much to me. Ignos has to work on its tactics —I've been torn away from my family, my empire, and all I've ever known and exposed to things I could never have dreamed of. Peace is nothing more than a joke to me now.

I make it to the bars, and as I do so, I see the creature's tongue uncurl from its mouth. The slathering pink tendril snakes its way around two of the bars and, as I watch, it shivers. The creature tenses.

Kaishi, you must listen to me. They mean you harm. These are not your friends!

There's a creaking snap and the two central bars of my cell bend inwards and then break in two. It's not much space to get through, and the jagged spikes of the broken bar ends keep me careful, but I make my way out to the balcony.

And look onto chaos.

What was, when we entered, an ordered set of routines is now a cascade of blown-open walls, frenzied firefights, and more than one up-close tussle between things I can't name. Even Ignos is too stunned to respond.

Then I feel the creature touch my arm. It's a cool, sliding sensation, like grabbing a jungle vine coated with morning dew. I shiver, and it grips me.

"You've taken too long already," the creature says, and its voice is a burbling brook, a rushing river. "My friends die now for your delay. We leave."

It's a command, not a question, and the thing pulls me away from the conflict playing out elsewhere. I stumble as it tugs, but my feet are well-versed in running and they find their steps quickly. Malo and Viera follow, though the creature doesn't pay them any attention; one of its black pupils is locked on me, the other ahead towards dangers unknown.

A few shouts harangue our run as we pass by unopened cells; those too unlucky to be part of the breakout. The creature pays them no mind, and I can't afford to as we're running now. I'm still wearing the mask from *Cobalt*, and it coats my feet as they stamp on the hard, smooth floor.

Fight back! To run with this one means death!

I can't help but hesitate at Ignos' words. The parasite hasn't ever tried to kill me, after all, even as it pursued its own ends.

The creature feels my pull, turns and glares at me. Its mouth comes to a point, and I realize there are a set of four tiny nostrils over the top of it, ones that flare at me now, coating my face with hot, sticky air. Then it cocks its head to the side, as if listening to a sound I cannot hear.

"You're the hosted one," the creature says.

"Yes, there's one inside me," I reply, though the creature doesn't seem to need the confirmation.

Ignos yells at me to run, thrashes in my head enough to make me wince. A gesture the creature notices.

"For the moment," the creature reaches into one of the many pockets of feathers coating its body, pulls out something I recognize: a long, thin metal fork.

"Hold her," the creature says to my friends.

I barely have a chance to react before Malo and Viera each grab an arm. Pin me back against them.

"Sorry, Kaishi, but neither of us has any love for that thing you've got with you," Viera says.

They used my miracles the same as you.

"You lied." I speak the words out loud without realizing.

The creature raising the fork pauses, then gives me a blink before continuing. Its feathered arm reaches up towards my head and I close my eyes, taking, for a moment, a chance to escape from what's about to happen. Ignos doesn't let me. It thrashes. Tickles and scratches my mind.

I'm your friend, Kaishi! Don't forget that I want you, your species to survive. Don't—

The connection breaks like a dry branch—a snap and then Ignos is gone from my mind. I feel it, though; gripped by the fork and pulled out from my ear and, with a wet splat, onto the floor next to me. The creature doesn't waste a moment; its tongue shoots out, wraps itself around the ghostly gray shell of Ignos and brings the parasite to its mouth.

"Don't," I say as Malo and Viera let my arms drop. "It's helped me. It brought us here."

"It's not coming with us," The creature replies, and it jerks its tongue a little farther into its mouth. "These things have no right to live."

"This one does." I reach into the creature's mouth, and as I grab Ignos, the creature relaxes its tongue.

I pull Ignos free—it feels both brittle and squishy in my hands, like a soft melon—and hold the Sevora. Ignos doesn't try to pull itself up my arms or scramble away from my hands. The life of the creature that tricked me, pushed me into a destiny I did not want, quivers in my palms.

"It gave our people freedom," Malo says behind me. "For whatever else it's done, the creature deserves mercy for that."

I nod. Then look over the great expanse from one side of cells to the other. The fights still rage, though I notice things are moving towards a retreat. Sevora guards, those furry Flaum moving in formation, are advancing, pushing back the motley squads of species I can't name.

"We must go," the creature says, and in its tone I gather the seconds remaining in Ignos' life are dwindling.

So I turn and throw the thing that's brought me here. That rescued my tribe from certain death and brought me to the heights of power. I aim with purpose, towards a group of Flaum advancing two floors below, miners keeping up a steady stream of fire. I see enough to know Ignos makes it across the gap, but before I see the result, my parasite and savior is gone.

Any chance I have to reflect on the moment is taken when the creature pulls me again, snarling that we're running out of time. Instinct takes over while my mind drifts in my suddenly quiet head as we sprint through dark hallways and down stairs.

Eventually we hit a landing covered with red-glowing runes that I can't understand. The creature seems to think there's another stair and wheels around, and we follow, only to find a thick sealed door blocking our path. The only other way is a broad, wide entry spanned by four archways. I can see bright beige sky out the other end, but when I take a step, the creature grabs my arm and pulls me back.

"There's nothing that way but death," the creature warbles, and then turns back to the door. "This shouldn't be shut."

"Don't know what your plan was," Viera says. "But that door isn't moving. Don't think we're going to like being on the other end of those miners either."

The Lunare steps up next to the creature, inspecting the door, and I take the chance to fall back near Malo.

"It's gone, Malo," I say, and the warrior knows what I'm talking about.

"Better that it is."

"You think so?" I look up at his face, and see its set in that too-serious way Malo has. As though he's about to deal with a cataclysm of terrific proportions, and only the most stoic of expressions can see him through. "Ignos helped us, a lot."

"A fruit, when ripe, is delicious. When rotten, poisonous. Ignos only helped you, I think, because it helped itself at the same time."

A bang ripples through the stairwell, from above. The creature stops staring at the door, shakes its head, and turns back, looking past Malo and I to the archways and the open air beyond.

"We're going to try for it," the creature says. "You're going to follow me, fast. Don't stop for anything, even when your body tells you it's going to die. Or you will."

Malo steps in front of me, but I pull myself around him, go up to the creature. Its deep green and black eyes meet mine, and when I extend my hand, its warm, rubbery grip meets it. The brilliant feathers streaming down the creature's arm make a pretty wing, though I wonder if it's quite big enough for flight. Certainly the creature's body is far larger than the eagles I know back home.

"We go together," I say to the creature, and to Malo. "Come on, you two."

The arch is split into sections by thin, dark rock bands—I can only see where those bands end because the pieces in between begin to glow a hard yellow. At the sight, the creature lunges forward and we do our best to keep up. It goes under the arch, padded feet flapping against the ground and I, with my hands on Malo and Viera's, follow. As we pass beneath the arch, I notice the next three are lighting up like the first.

"Don't stop!" the creature cries.

I don't see anything that's going to prevent me; there's no wall, no rope around my ankles or armed guard. But there is, as I pass beneath the arch, a prickling sensation that crawls over my skin. Like getting lightly scratched by thorns all across my body. I think the mask I'm wearing blunts, but doesn't stop the sensation.

We don't stop.

Out the other side of the arch the feeling disappears. Arch number two, apparently cued, shifts its glow from yellow to a sickly orange, like a sunset trying to fight through clouds. The creature doesn't pause, but keeps going.

"Didn't like that," Viera says as we keep after it.

"It wasn't that bad," I reply.

"Then why have it at all?"

I can't answer that, because we're going through the second arch and the orange glow makes itself known immediately. Like diving into a hot bath, it's an instant change from the cool air of the hallway to a scalding rake across my body. I feel like when I was young, dared to dart across a fire, and my leap didn't carry me far enough—the flames licked me then as they seem to now.

I don't see fire. I feel it. The puckering of my skin, the air that I breathe stinging my throat. The mask lets me get just enough to keep going, keeps me from passing out.

We move, the three of us, and then we're through. I feel Malo begin to let up, feel myself suck in mouthfuls of air, and I know that I would give anything for water in that moment.

"You cannot stop!" it's the creature, and it's still moving towards the next arch, which is shining a crimson red.

"This thing has lost its mind," Malo says. "It wants us dead."

"We don't have a choice." I push past the pain in my legs, force myself onward.

When the creature enters the third arch, there's a burst of light and it takes a moment for me to realize that its feathers are actually on fire. The tips burn as it moves, and its blue-green skin glistens as it hardens, chars.

Then I see nothing because my own eyelashes alight. My hair burns, along with the robes I'm wearing, though I notice those only as curious after-thoughts, a sort of addition to the sheer chaos of my own nerves as the mask barely keeps my skin from melting. Yet, as hot as this is, as scalding and brutal, I drift back to the endless series of struggles I'd braved to get here. All the dangers, all the near-deaths. A little bit of fire isn't going to stop me. Not now.

My right hand, singing its pain, nonetheless tells me when Viera falls. I can't see—I've closed my eyes to keep the heat from melting them—but I reach and feel the Lunare on the ground. Grab her searing shoulder and pull. Feel Malo yanking me ahead.

When my left arm leaves the arch, it's like falling into the cold ocean. Immediate ice, comforting and cool. Every piece of me that follows is a rapture, an ecstasy that doesn't slip back to aching pain until all of me is out, until I've dragged Viera's burning self into the gap between arches.

I start patting the Lunare immediately, batting at her with what remain of mine and her clothes, and then a pair of webbed hands join the effort, and we get the small fires put out quick. Viera's still conscious, but she's shaky as she rises back to her feet.

"Can't do that again," she says, and her voice is scratched, harsh.

"You won't need to," the creature replies.

It pulls out the small miner I'd seen it holding earlier. Then draws the other one. The last arch is glowing a purple-black. I can't imagine what could be worse than what we've already experienced, and the thought of braving something else makes me shiver.

The thing hurls one of its miners towards the last arch. As the weapon reaches one of the glowing sections, the creature aims and fires its other miner. The shot strikes the thrown weapon as it nears the top of the arch, exploding the projectile in a blast of bright white and green flares. The top of the arch crumples and crackles with a bang, and chunks of it fall to the ground in front of us. Sparks pop and sizzle from the severed remnants.

"Couldn't you have done that earlier?" Viera says.

"Only have two miners," the creature replies, bearing its new scars without complaint. "Had to save them for the last arch. The one that would've killed you had you tried to go through it."

"Just about killed us anyway," Viera mutters as the creature steps over the wreckage and through the apparently safe arch.

We follow, and the thick doors to the outside recoil like a fan, pressing back into each other through to the side as we near. The hall opens into a vast courtyard; a tiled expanse marked by large smooth patches where, it's not hard to imagine, some of the many ships shooting through the sky might set down.

The creature waves us forward, and we leave the doorway, taking all of five steps before we notice the forms pressed against the building behind us. Flaum, ten of them, in all manner of browns, blacks, whites and grays. They're holding miners, and they point them at us, though most aim at the creature. They look just like Nasiya's Flaum, our guards from earlier, except for one thing: the badges on their chests. Not the green and black circle but instead a blue and yellow mixture. Colors racing together like paints dropped on a stone.

My eyes flick back to the creature, and it's hesitating. Its hand is on the one miner it has left, but I don't believe it's going to fight. It would be stupid, impossible. If it tried, I have no doubt we would be burned to oblivion.

"Don't shoot," I say. "Nobody needs to die here."

A bit of the Empress is still left in me, even without Ignos. I'm still trying to save the lives of my subjects, all two of them.

"If the Dawn goes, then we won't need to shoot anybody," one of the Flaum, a speckled white and black one, says.

Its miner, a thick and long rifle, points directly at the creature, who proceeds to heed the warning, to drop its own weapon onto the stone with a loud clatter.

"They're yours, then," the creature says. "I expect a thank-you."

"You'll get one, when we're finished with them."

The Flaum never flinches. Never takes the miner away. Not until the creature, without a look back at us, bounds away across the stone and vanishes through a wide gate in an outer wall.

I notice one of the other Flaum tapping something into an armlet on his wrist. I keep my eyes on it, even as the rest the Flaum fan out around us. Encircle us, and aim their weapons outside.

"From one prison to another," Viera says.

"We'll find our way out of the next one too," I say. "We just need to stay together."

Malo grips my hand, strong. Calm. What I need him to be right now. The emptiness in my head remains a terrifying vacuum, and I wish I could ask Ignos what these badges mean. Who these things are. Ignos, though, isn't here. It might be dead, and I don't dare slip into the Cache's knockout knowledge now.

I feel the air before I hear the sound. A rush of blowing wind, bringing with it smells I don't recognize. Unnatural ones; chemicals and burning things. I follow the Flaum's stares and look up in time to see an elegant, bizarre craft descending down towards us. It's a long, flat surface curved around the sides and bottom; a shallow oval. Like the badges, it too is painted in bright blues and yellows, and also reds and blacks all mixing together as if the thing simply exploded out of a rainbow.

"You have a weird sense of style," Viera says to the only Flaum that's spoken, the speckled one.

"We stand by our principles," the Flaum replies. "All things together, all things inseparable."

"What do you want with us?" I try to ask, but the Flaum ignores me.

No, the Sevora that controls it ignores me. I can't forget that we're on a world of parasites. That all of these things have, like Ignos, a controlling monster inside of them.

We don't have a choice, so we follow the Flaum over and up the ramp, into the craft. The floors are white, the same pearl as the tubes and elsewhere and it's not long before we feel it mold around our feet. Keep us tethered to the ground and stabilized. The same thing happens to the Flaum, though most manage to keep their weapons angled our way as the ship ascends back to the sky. As it moves, the plain walls and ceiling fade, turn translucent, as if I'm looking through smeared glass.

Frenzied movement outside keeps my attention as we fly away from the prison. Larger ships are moving towards where we just left, and I see more than a few smaller craft take tentative slides towards our ship before breaking off. Small dots that I assume are more troops descend from the larger, blocky ships and stream towards the prison like ants.

Part of me hopes the creature escapes, the other part isn't sure.

The ship arcs over the city, higher and higher yet not quite into the black of space. I feel the craft accelerate, move fast and burst away from where we were.

"Where are we going?" I yell to the speckled Flaum, as none of the others have shown any interest in talking.

"To safety," the Flaum replies. "To another part of Vimelia, where Nasiya won't be able to find you."

So Nasiya doesn't know about this. Interesting.

Back on Earth, in Damantum, I'd had a bit of experience playing politics. In the weeks after the Emperor's death, after my own ascension, I'd come to know the various factions of the city. Come to taste their squabbles and grow irritated with their endless demands, most of which had little to do with aiding their people and much more to do with hurting those they feared. Or thought were their enemies.

There's something else I learned in those weeks: that divisions, turmoil, can be exploited.

The flight doesn't last long. While it's hard to tell time on a planet that doesn't seem to have a true night, I think it's less than an hour. Just as my feet start to hurt, and my knees quiver at staying in the same position, we descend. It's a straight down drop that leads to a gentle landing on a wide pad, like the prison. However, unlike the metal constructs and bustling buildings of the city we were in, this place is lush and green.

It's not hard to see why: small discs covered in nozzles buzz around every meter of open space, sending long sweeping arcs of what looks like water on to groves of flowers, trees, and grasses. Long thin tubes trail from the discs back to some underground reservoir. It's a bigger, more wondrous garden than anything I've ever seen. Plants, or least I think that's what I think they are, spiral up and around and grow out in all directions. Some appear to be solid glass, while others look to be pulsing, like a heart soon after it's freed from its human prison. A grove next to me shoots silver trunks straight up stories into the air before, at the top, bursting into a fluted nova of pink and red flowers. Others, dome-shaped, open every few seconds and release a tingly blue spray into the air. As we walk, escorted by the Flaum, I catch some and think of mint and jasmine.

There's music here too, though I'm not sure from where it comes. Or if, really, it's music at all. It's almost like a chant, a low rhythm that nonetheless rises and falls to some beat and measure only the player knows. I find my feet matching its echoes as we move along a wide, white gravel path towards what I think is a building far too small for such a magnificent display.

It's a singular tower, though not much taller than my village's Tier. And not much wider either. As we draw close, the speckled Flaum holds up a hand and we all stop. I've learned that signal by now. The Flaum waves in front of us towards the tower and as he gestures, I see the air around the tower shimmer. Like peeling back a shroud, the tower elongates and grows wider and wider until it's the width of what the garden lets me see and maybe more. It grows higher until its taller than the trees of my jungle. Taller than several of them stacked on one another.

"We keep our strength hidden," the speckled Flaum offers without our asking.

The door, however, stays the same size and so, with three Flaum in front and three behind, we walk through in a line. What we come to is not a place of power like the throne room in my old palace, but instead a ringing mess. A chaos of shouting voices, a crowd of Flaum and other species of all kinds and names I don't know yelling and screaming and buzzing at each other. Every once in a while I see something fly through the air; small rocks aimed at someone across the wide room.

The floor gently slopes down so that whomever is the object of all the shouting stands at the middle. Up above, balconies ring the vast space, and even more species lean over the edges, haranguing in their loud voices. I've never heard such a roar, so much clashing of tongues, and my first thought is to put my hands up to my ears and press, closing my eyes. To quiet, just for a moment, the noise.

At first I think I've been too effective. The shouts all die away, and then I hear nothing. It's only when I open my eyes do I realize that faces of every shape and color look towards me, Malo, and Viera. As if interpreting a signal, the speckled Flaum waves us forward, points to the dais in the middle, on which stands a great, blotched orange slug. Unlike the slimy things of my home, this one has arms, this one wears clothes, and this one grins at me with toothless pride as I make my way through the crowd towards it.

"Here we have our prize," the slug thing gurgles as we draw close. "The very thing Nasiya sought to keep from us. The proof of our position, of the necessity of peace."

Bas isn't here. It's the first thing Sax notices, it's what he focuses on. A pair finds his pair.

The room is a circle, and he's not in the middle but bunched up on one of the sides. A pair of the mud-like creatures are sitting in the center, playing some sort of game on a table. They look over as Sax begins to stir.

"Wake up? Almost too late," the one speaking gravel is a clay color, the other one a brown mud. "Boss say to kill you in an hour."

"Oratus too rare to kill. Boss was joking." The mud one lurches up from the seat, bits of itself sticking behind it.

Bits that will regrow.

Sax blinks a few times. Reasserts his vision. Pushes his vents to inhale and test the air; clean, but not so pure as on the ship. Space stations, even the ones with the best recyclers, have too much air and too much smell to handle to get the same quality as a small vessel. And *Scrapper Station* doesn't have top-tier parts. What Sax gets is the scent of booze, of chemicals and sweat. More than a little bit of blood. Makes his claws tingle. Makes them want to add to it.

But if there's one thing he doesn't want to fight, it's these two. Whatever body lies beneath that rocky exterior is going to take a lot to get to, and there's more than a little chance of his claws breaking off as Sax tries to dig through that thick skin. So Sax sits up instead. Glances around the plain art in the room; vistas pulled from various planets and stuck around, without any unifying theme or purpose. As if someone simply grabbed what they could find and threw it against the wall. Like *Scrapper Station* itself.

"Where's Bas?" Sax hisses.

There's no headache. No lingering pain. They gave him meds, made sure the Oratus wasn't too badly hurt. Which means they're not thinking he'll be a captive for long. They want to use him.

"Fine," the clay one says. "Awake. Working."

"Doing what?"

"Business," Brown says. "Your job too. Keep people honest."

"We're part of the Vincere," Sax replies. "We're not your tools. We're not your peons, your employees, your guards. You'll let us go, or when the rest of the Vincere arrive, you'll be blown to particles so small nothing in this place will get any use out of you."

They laugh; a low rumble, like boulders falling and clashing against one another. Perhaps, Sax thinks, that's because that's what it is. Rock and earth grinding together. Sax is starting to believe, though, that his threats are losing power. He hasn't managed to get a single one to work lately. Dalachite on *Cobalt* certainly didn't care, neither did the Lunare on Earth, or even the Sevora on that seed ship. The Oratus aren't what they used to be.

"Save threats for boss," the clay one rumbles. "You, us, the same. Stuck."

Sax can't help but wonder if this is what they've been fighting for. All those Oratus that have given themselves, all the Flaum and Whelk supporting them, for these lumps of rock who can't do anything more than spout nihilistic nonsense. Stuck.

Not for much longer.

"Take me to this boss," Sax says, not bothering to address the clay one's remarks. "I'm guessing he'll want to see me."

This time it's the brown one that takes the lead, "Us give tour, first."

Sax waves a claw. Doesn't object. Might as well see if there's anything worth knowing about *Scrapper Station* before he tears it apart.

The two Lutos lead Sax out of the room, and instead of another long, featureless hallway, the room opens right out to a wide floor. It's a big space, connected to others by half-closed walls with sloping doors. Mirrors drape those walls, casting back reflections of gambling tables and video displays. And those entrapped by them. The sounds of laughter and curses, cheers and jeers echo. Sax is in a place he despises, a place that thrives on chance and making odds against those who choose to partake. It is the antithesis of what the Oratus believe; that preparation can make victory certain.

Like a magnet for his eyes, Sax feels his gaze slide to the right, to a cluster of rollerball tables—where the contestants all take turns pitching colored orbs against a vast target board. The scores change depending on where the balls land, and whomever happens to find themselves with the highest one wins while the others lose and, of course, the house takes a cut. A little bit of skill, a lot of luck, and Bas looks like she's had about enough of it. Sax's pair looms over the bundle of Whelk playing at the tables. Their liquid-like bodies fling the balls one after another, and Sax is compelled to go over there, but the the rock monsters grab his arms and lead him on.

"Later," the clay one rumbles. "You both stay, anyway."

Bas gives Sax a slight nod, and that's all Sax needs to know. She's safe, bored but okay. Which means he can focus on his two escorts, and where they're leading him.

It turns out the gambling hall isn't all that big. One more small room and they're out, back into the basic interior of the dilapidated station. Sax can still see all the marks where different plates were welded together, pieces scrapped from various wrecks forced into place. A habitat made with the ghosts of others. The core of *Scrapper Station* is a large open space dotted with tables, benches, people hawking goods and an endless swarm of species in transition from hopeful to hopeless and back again.

Gravity here comes from the spinning, and Sax can feel it in his talons as they grip the metal. A slight shifting, as if his stomach were in a wind tunnel. In here, outside the gambling hall, they're in the center, where the gravity's the strongest. Spokes shoot away from this core in all directions.

"How many live here?" Sax asks to get them talking, revealing something, maybe, he can use.

"Thousand," Clay says. "More free here, than working for Amigga."

"Hah," Brown replies. "Your idea to come here. Now we're stuck. Watching baby Oratus."

"Baby?" Sax hisses.

The Lutos don't answer and the conversation's over.

They take a walk around the core, with the rock monsters pointing out the way to residential spokes, bars, restaurants, docking bays and the cluster of other services. Medical, waste, manufacturing are all bundled together in their own spokes. *Scrapper Station* seems a little too well ordered for a place way out here, without an Amigga to run it.

"Ooblots manage things," the clay one says. "Bosses' sisters."

That explains it then. Ooblots are always organized, dedicated. Weak and cowardly. Sax has never met one himself, not counting just a few hours ago. Never wanted to.

Now the Lutos are telling him it's time. Back to the gambling hall, through a door on the far end. Sax tries to catch another sight of Bas, but she's not looking; busy with some dispute. Her claws ready. Sax wants to watch, both in case he needs to help, and because there's something about watching his pair work that's entrancing. But he doesn't get the chance. He's ushered through and this time there is a short hallway. To the right and left Sax can see the rooms where security is monitoring everything. In the back is what he's expecting; the lush luxury that Ooblots are known for.

There's a couple of eye stalks standing from the creature as it sits on a velvet red couch. Like a Whelk with an added helping of liquidity, the Ooblot puddles himself around the surface. The skin that Sax thought was yellow is, on inspection, closer to gray with plenty of golden blotches from radiation—too much time on *Scrapper Station* and its poorly shielded hull.

"Sax, right? I am D'Rascale, what do you think of my little enterprise?" The Ooblot says, and its voice is a slap-smack of liquid thwacks as the Ooblot hardens and softens its body, throwing parts of it against itself to make the words.

"It's a pile of garbage," Sax replies and bares his teeth, just a little.

"Honesty. I can appreciate that. We all can, especially in a place like this, where lies often travel farther than the truth," D'Rascale doesn't get up, doesn't wave for Sax to move anywhere.

Just stares at him with those two large round eyes set in those stalks.

A long breath of silence. The two Lutos still have hold of Sax's arms, and the grip is tighter now than it was outside. They think he's going to attack. That he's going to fly into some sort of rage. Sax wants to, but his pair is out there. He wouldn't be doing Bas any favors by getting himself killed here.

"They tell you?" D'Rascale asks.

"I don't have time for games," Sax says. "I don't have time to work for you. An Oratus is not a security guard, a janitor, or whatever else you have in mind. We are warriors, we belong at the front. You will hail the Vincere, and you will let us go until they arrive. In exchange, you will be rewarded."

The Ooblot swings a tendril out wide and, as if by magic, a small servo robot putters over and hands D'Rascale a small drink. The Ooblot places its newly-formed appendage over the lip, and from the center of its 'hand' a pipe-link tube emerges and descends into the liquid, sucking it up with a slurping noise.

Sax eyes the beverage. The last thing he's had to eat or drink was back on *Cobalt*. He was too distracted on Plake's ship, and now his body, sensing a chance to feed itself, awakens.

"It seems you do need something," D'Rascale says, its left eye rotating on its stalk to focus on Sax's face. No, beneath his lips, where, Sax realizes, a bit of saliva has snaked itself out and is making its final escape towards the floor.

Sax catches the drop in his right mid-claw. He's not an animal.

"Your Vincere, if you are so necessary as you claim, will no doubt come for you," D'Rascale continues. "Until they arrive, we can strike a deal. You work for me, I feed you." A dwindling pause. "Your pair agreed to it."

"Liar." Bas would never agree to something like this. Would never accept servitude, no matter the price.

"She mentioned you might react this way. But here's the truth, Oratus. You're stuck here and you have two choices: either you work for me, do as I say and reap the benefits or I have these two throw you out an airlock so you can have the death you so obviously wish for."

"Is it me that wishes for death?" Sax hisses and then hurls forward, jabbing with his foreclaws and slipping their sharp edges beneath the Ooblot's slippery body. With his tail batting back the two rock monsters, Sax lifts the creature above his head, then tilts his mouth up and opens wide, so D'Rascale can see just how many teeth will be cutting into him.

But the Ooblot seems unfazed. D'Rascale takes another drink from the glass, still held in its sucking hand.

"This is why you'd be such a good fit here," the Ooblot says. If being an inch away from death has any effect on the creature, Sax doesn't see it now. "In fact—"

There's a shout, then another and a crash from outside the room. Back towards the casino floor. Back towards Bas

Sax doesn't hesitate; he drops D'Rascale block back on the couch, turns and barges his way up through the door. Down the short hallway and onto a casino floor that's broken into chaos. Tables are overturned, species are running wildly, and Bas in the middle of it all, her pink-gold tail thrashing what looks like one of the Whelks away from her and sending it flying. Two more slug creatures try to pile her to the ground while another tears the end off of a bar chair and begins to bring it over.

Begins.

Sax provides the end.

He takes two long steps and then presses his talons to the ground and launches himself over the large bar in the middle of the floor. He clips some bottles, sends a few glasses tumbling, but the Oratus makes it across in time to catch the advancing Whelk in mid-swing. His claws dive into the gel-like surface of the slug-creature's skin, digging and scooping and gripping and then he's throwing the Whelk away.

What should have been a mortal wound for most species hardly fazes the Whelk, and it catches itself on the floor, rolls, and then it wriggles its way upright. You want to kill a Whelk, you have to pierce an organ or cut them all the way in half.

This one, though, with its yellow green skin and wild eyes, doesn't come charging back. It hesitates, and in that moment Bas turns the odds even further against the slugs. She throws the two things off her—both slamming against the wall next to the rollerball tables—and rises up behind Sax. Now faced with two ready, angry Oratus, the four Whelk decide they've already lost enough and run from the room.

"I want them banned," D'Rascale says, its voice slapping as it slides into the room. "This is the third time those four have decided to end their night damaging my floor. Look how much business I've lost. If it weren't for the two of you, it might've been even worse."

Sax is about to reply that he was just protecting his pair when D'Rascale holds up a flat hand. "I'm not asking for a commitment right this moment. Take a breath, have some dinner. Then tell me if you'd prefer to die, or work." The Ooblot gestures back to the room he just came from; apparently that's the Oratus' temporary refuge.

As much as Sax wishes he could tear D'Rascale apart, he realizes a good choice when he sees one. If he's hungry and tired, then Bas probably is as well. A chance to talk in private, a chance to be away for a moment from people that want them in servitude, would be nice.

"Take him up on it," Bas hisses quietly. "For once, put your pride aside and give us a moment."

Bas settles it. Sax isn't going to go against his pair. He's far too tired for that.

The Lutos don't say a word as the two Oratus retreat to the refuge of the room. The servo robot brings them water and food. Nutrient goop, but also some fresh grown vegetables. Sax stares at the leafy green, likely produced from hydroponics here on the station. It's such a rarity that Sax overlooks his usual distaste for things that aren't bleeding and instead delights in the crisp crunchy flavor.

Only after they've consumed several pounds of food apiece do the two Oratus settle back on the red couch and look at each other. There's no more avoiding it.

"We can't stay," Sax says. "I won't work for him. I won't work for anybody."

"We've been taking orders our entire lives Sax," Bas replies. "What does it matter if we're taking orders from an Ooblot instead of Evva?"

"You just said it yourself. It's not Evva. It's not the Vincere. This isn't who we are."

Bas turns her rose-gold head away, stares at the mirrored walls. Clicks her claws. "We're weapons, Sax. And weapons are wielded. We've just changed hands, is all."

Sax is about to reply. To snarl and suggest they break their way out right now. Clearly, what Bas needs is a real fight, not the dusting they had a moment ago. Something to remind her of who she is.

A crackling from an intercom breaks his momentum.

"Sorry for disturbing you, but I feel there is something you should know. It's coming in off the broad waves." The Ooblot doesn't say anything more as a screen descends from the room ceiling. It turns on to reveal a familiar face.

Evva. Reddish-black scales. Next to her, a long list of apparent crimes.

It takes a while for the sound to arrive, for the broadcast to begin to play, and as with anything transmitted over the relays, it's a grainy, simple sound. But Sax doesn't need fancy audio to discern the words.

Evva, traitor to the Oratus, to the Chorus, plotter of dangerous crimes and spreader of false rumors, is declared a danger to the galaxy. Any who see her should take all precautions and contact the nearest authorities to ensure this stain on our society is dealt with.

The Whelk calls itself Jel, and it escorts us out of the chamber when the cheering dies away to fast conversation. Jel, however, brings its own conversation with us, warbling away as we wind through yet another nest of halls. I should feel claustrophobic—most of the buildings of my childhood were open constructs without these narrow corridors—but I'm struck by the art on display.

The Solare, my tribe and kin, use paints from flowers, fruits, and crushed rock to illustrate our history on our towering Tiers, tattoos on our skin, and dyes on the furs and mossweaves that make up our clothes. A form of expression we've refined over many generations. One I find beautiful.

And yet.

These hallways *ripple*. That's the only word I can think of for how the streams of color dart and dance with one another as we walk. They aren't images, really, but abstract bursts in constant motion, twirling and mixing and splashing their bright reds, yellows, and blues all across the space. I've seen screens now, both on the shuttle here and the space station *Cobalt*, and these appear more natural, not the product of glowing light.

"Each and every one represents a race in this galaxy," Jel shifts its speech suddenly, its big, bulbous head shifting towards me. "Their dance is the same one we perform even now, coming together and apart again."

"It's beautiful," I say, and know the words are inadequate.

"Notice how they never break one another?"

I'm about to answer when Viera does for me. "That's what you're all about, right? No war? Everyone plays nice?"

Jel nods, or maybe bows; it's difficult to tell when the Whelk's head essentially molds right onto its body. Jel slithers on and we follow. This time, when the Whelk resumes its speech, I try to listen.

Nasiya's faction, Jel says, are called the Hasir. They run Vimelia, and their constant agitation for Sevora independence, war and pride is the source of their power and the Sevora's overall decline. The Wem, of whom Jel is the elected leader, would see treaties. Would see reconnecting with the galaxy at large.

The words become a jumble as more species and organizations tumble out of Jel's mouth and, despite myself, I tune Jel out again and focus on the more visceral differences I'm seeing between here and Nasiya's buildings. First and foremost, the Wem seem to be fans of yellower, softer light. The glow suffuses everything, though I'm never quite sure where it comes from. As we leave the swirling paints behind and enter what appears to be some form of dormitory, the gold bricks that make up the place have their own luminescence. I brush my hand on one of the shining stones and glance at my fingers; they're coated with a fine dust that, like a far off star, twinkles.

Every breath I take, too, brings with it flowery perfume from the gardens outside, smells that take me back to the jungle, and ones far different from the sterile efficiency of the Hasir buildings. A constant, soft breeze keeps the air moving and the temperature cooler than I'd like, but not so cold that I'm uncomfortable. Viera looks right at home, while Malo, like me, rubs his arms as we move.

"Not all the Wem stay here," Jel is saying, gesturing with a stubby green arm up at the rows of rooms. "Most who do use this as a temporary refuge, to get away from the chaos of the city."

"Or to hide from a crime?" Viera asks.

I give the Lunare a sharp glance, but Jel's laugh cuts any embarrassment.

"If necessary," Jel says. "We try to keep as much of our work out of the grime as we can, but sometimes change requires a sleight hand."

"And gray morals," Viera adds.

"You will starve on virtue alone," Jel acknowledges. "Still, we are not Clarity's Dawn. We do not seek to destroy, only change."

The title tickles a memory, but before I can ask a question, we're moving again. The rooms, unlike the cells in the prison, open onto vine-wrapped balconies, and a pair of waterfalls trickle down on either side of a wide, tan platform that we board. At ground level around us, tall trees rise, sporting long tendrils ending in bright pink blooms. As soon as Malo steps on the platform, Jel does something I don't catch and the platform begins to rise.

Viera snares Jel in conversation and I take the opportunity to slide near Malo and ask him what he thinks.

"In these last days, Kaishi, I have seen more wonders than I thought possible," Malo says, but his voice carries caution with it, and I note that he's speaking Charre, not the so-called common language used by every species we've seen so far.

"But?"

"Everyone we've met appears to want to use us for something. I can't believe these 'Wem' will be any different."

I chew on that for a second. Malo's right, of that I don't have any doubt. Nobody, not even my father and my tribe, would treat visitors with so much hospitality unless there was something they believed they would get in return.

"Malo, I'm starting to believe that's what our lives are," I say. "When we were young, we had to obey our elders, our superiors, and, above them, our gods. This isn't all that different."

The platform continues up, past the rooms and still higher, above the top of the chamber and into a tunnel bordered on all sides by those glowing bricks.

"There's a difference being told what to do by your parents, by the people you trust, or the gods you worship. They, at least, care about you. These things? Kaishi, I feel they would throw us away in a moment if we were of no use to them."

"You think they could throw us away? You? Warrior of the Charre?"

I mean the words to bulk up Malo's spirit, bring a laugh or a smile to his face, but all I get is a grimace.

"I couldn't protect you back on Earth. I didn't save you on *Cobalt*. Why think I can protect you here?"

"Because you promised me," I reply. "And my general doesn't break promises."

That, at least, gets a rueful grin. A small nod of thanks.

The ceiling parts above us and the platform breaks out into the open air. We're on top of the huge building, on a spire that rises over the main roof. Glass encircles us, and I can see, around the sandy ground, the circular garden spreading out around the structure. Beyond the green, buildings rise up, though in a more patchwork fashion than the concentrated metropolis we first landed in.

"Vimelia's city never truly ends," Jel says as we take in the view. "But it does quiet from time to time. We chose this place precisely because it sits beyond the clamber, because it forces us to see natural beauty. Remind ourselves that we strive for nature's harmony, not a forced structure."

"How?" I ask. "You talk about taking over the Sevora, about changing your species, but how? The Hasir, and Nasiya, seem to have so much more than you."

"The Sevora blow like a leaf in this eternal wind," Jel replies. "A strong gust in our direction could, in one stroke, give us the planet. I hope that gust will be you."

"Never been a gust before," Viera says. "Do I wave my arms like this?"

The Lunare sweeps her hands from side to side and I roll my eyes. Malo looks away, shaking his head. Jel, though, says nothing, and Viera, seeing nobody appreciating her jest, settles into a humph.

"No, there is one thing that must happen before we go any farther," Jel says, and by the sudden weight in its tone, I can tell our happy tour is at an end. "We have members who have earned their chance to make a difference. Earned a chance to try. Earned a host such as yourselves."

There's a heavy silence.

One I break.

"You want to infect us."

"This is the Sevora home, human," Jel says. "To be here, you must be one of us."

"Ignos couldn't control me," I reply, the thought of another creature in my head injecting acid into my voice. "Your Sevora won't get what they want."

"One test does not make a thorough experiment," Jel replies, and I notice now that its two hands have slipped beneath its strange robe. It's not difficult to imagine a miner or two hiding beneath those folds. "Either we will prove you are not all you claim to be, and gain a new host species, or we will have the guides in place to ensure you know what to say and when to say it."

"Not happening," I say. Malo shifts behind me, getting ready. Viera, too, faces Jel, her hands loose. "I'm not letting any of you in my head ever again."

I have no idea if Jel understands my words—the Whelk sits there, its gooey mass playing about like a line of drippy tree sap. Malo and Viera take up positions on either side of me, and now it's the three of us on one side of the platform, and Jel on the other. Viera, who a moment ago had seemingly been the best of friends with Jel, wears the hardest expression of us; pure loathing etches into her face and I'm very glad the Lunare's with me instead of the other way around.

"Again?" Jel asks. "I didn't know any of you had the joy of being a host before?"

"It wasn't intentional," I reply.

The platform judders, then begins to descend back into the building. For a moment, I think our shot at escape vanishes with those glass walls, but we don't have any tools to break them with anyway.

"And now you are *unhosted*," Jel says the word the same way I might say 'diseased'.

"We're free, if that's what you mean," Viera speaks up. "We're staying that way too. So find another way to prove your point, or let us go."

The glowing bricks again surround us, locking the tension into that little platform.

"The Sevora will never listen to one that isn't a part of us," Jel says, and it tucks its arms back beneath the robes. "It would not have to be a permanent situation, but at first, it will be necessary."

Jel makes a certain sort of sense—I don't think the Solare or the Charre tribes back on Earth would listen to Viera without me or Malo vouching for her. But there's a wide chasm between supporting someone and letting a creature infest your mind.

"Necessary for you," I say. "We have no stake in your fight. All we want is a ship off this planet and back to ours."

Viera shoots me a look and I realize I've made a mistake. Given away something we need, and by the way Jel quivers —a motion which sends a side of my stomach twisting—the Whelk caught it.

"Ships can be arranged," Jel replies slowly. "Our planet is, however, engaged in a long-running, costly war. Sparing a vessel to take you home would require resources. Would need payment. I think you know how to deliver that."

The platform keeps moving and scenarios play out like lightning in my mind; if I agree with the creature, we submit, and they stick their friends inside us. If things go well, and Jel's faction gets what they want, why would they bother letting us go? If it goes poorly, then Nasiya has us all killed or stuffed with his own Sevora.

I don't have to look at Malo and Viera to know they've reached the same conclusion.

"Take it," I say in the Charre tongue. "Jel's our only way out of here."

Malo moves faster than I think possible; he dives forward, his shoulder slamming into Jel's bulk while his hands scrabble for its arms, trying to keep them from drawing whatever the Whelk has in its pockets. Jel utters a surprised warble as it hits the bricks going by, and almost gets its left arm free before Viera arrives. The Lunare tears the small miner from Jel's grip and places the weapon up close towards Jel's huge head.

"Or," I say. "You can give it to us to be nice. That's what friends do, right?"

The platform sinks beneath the bricks and back into the large dormitory. The first chance we'll have of being discovered, and it's a chance we immediately lose: there's plenty of creatures walking across the balconies, waiting for the platform, or chattering with one another. It only takes a single loud burble from Jel before plenty of types of eyes turn our way.

"I'm thinking we'll be running from this one," Viera says.

"We use the hostage." Malo adjusts his grip and his hands dig deeper into Jel's apparently soft skin.

"You're only hurting my host," Jel says, its voice suddenly tight, and I wonder if Malo's squeezing the thing that allows the Whelk to talk. "You'll only kill the Whelk. You have no leverage, except a surrender."

"Throw it," I say.

The platform's just about at the highest floor of the dormitory, the one with the fewest gawkers on it. We'll be dead or captured if we stay here in the open—I learned that much in the jungle.

Malo obeys, giving Viera a moment to shift back to my side, and then, with Jel protesting, he shoves the Whelk forward against the platform's railing. The Charre warrior grunts, squats, and starts to lift Jel over as the platform settles onto the third floor landing.

We're out of time.

"Cover us!" I shout to Viera, and I dash forward, planting my hands against Jel's body as Malo lifts the squirming Whelk over the railing.

Jel's skin is cold, clammy, and altogether disgusting—like grabbing a rotting fruit from a puddle, but my shove is enough to tip Jel over the edge, toppling the Whelk off the platform and down towards the ground floor. It strikes with a wet splat, and I turn away from the carnage. Part of me notes that I've just killed another species for the first time, and I quash any guilty thoughts by reminding myself that the Whelk lost itself to the Sevora long ago.

"Take another step and I'll shoot you. And you. Several times." Viera's threats accompany Malo and I off the platform and onto the wide balcony that wraps around the level.

A pair of confused Flaum, hands empty and wearing the same robe as Jel, face us. Those badges are there too, the painted ones. If these Flaum, or, really, the Sevora controlling them, have any courage, however, it vanishes when they look down to see what's become of their leader. Both of them slide against the wall and wave us by.

We go.

We have no plan, no idea of how to get out, but we move. My feet pound against the hard floor and I throw glances at every room we run past, looking for some way down or out. Mostly, I have no idea what I'm looking at. One has a series of nets hanging from the ceiling. Another a pool of purple-black ink in the ground, and the third looks like a miniature flower garden, though many of the blossoms have been eaten.

"What are these things?" I say without realizing it.

"No idea," Viera huffs in front of me. "Is it bad that I kind of want to stay here and figure that out?"

"It's your choice." Malo replies from the back.

Shouts follow us now from below, and I've no doubt the platform is moving down to the ground to pick up someone armed with more than fear. We're almost at the end of this side, and I'm hoping that something shows up soon or this escape attempt is going to be real short-lived. Already, looking back, I see a half-dozen Flaum pouring off of the platform and starting after us.

We hit the back wall of the level and there's nothing there. Another room on our right, and the balcony continues around in a long U that will only bring us to the people we're trying to avoid. I hear a pop, and see Malo's holding a miner now too. Another small one, just like Viera's. His shot goes wide of the approaching force, but they duck down into cover.

"They're not shooting back," Viera says as she presses me down behind the railing.

"Because we're only valuable to them alive," I reply, my eyes stuck on Malo's miner.

Idea.

"Give me your miner," I tell Viera, and the Lunare hesitates. "I said give it to me."

This time I inject my best empress tone, the one that suggests all sorts of terrible things if I don't get what I want. Viera, understands and hands over her weapon without complaint. As soon as I get my fingers around the hilt, I turn and, yelling Malo's name, throw the miner across the space between us and the Wem guards.

Malo gets it.

Aims.

Shoots.

Everyone's watching my thrown miner, the guards with confused disbelief, and thus everyone sees Malo's shot miss and bury itself into the side wall splitting a pair of rooms. I'm about to panic as one of the guards catches the miner with its furry Flaum hand, aims it back at us

—

Malo fires again.

I can tell he doesn't miss because everything flares staccato white for a moment and there's a rippling sound, like a massive scroll of paper being torn again and again. Heat washes over me in waves as I fall back against the wall, away from the balcony. My nose stings—who knows what I'm breathing in, but it's not natural.

When the fire doesn't die right away, when the bangs roll over us in waves, I realize this isn't what I expected. I'd thrown one miner, but our whole level is shaking.

Oh wait. The guards. They must have been carrying their own weapons.

I open my eyes slow. Blink away the smoke. Look to where the guards stood a moment ago and there's only charred remnants of a balcony there. A concave divot splits the gap, those glowing bricks looking awful black now. I can't see any sign of the guards and I don't look too hard because I'm going to have enough nightmares as it is.

"Let's go," Viera says, and I'm only too happy to jump up to my feet, but hesitate when she goes back by Malo, towards the gap.

"Wrong way?" I venture.

"You just gave us our stairs," Viera points and while I wouldn't go so far as to call the wreckage 'stairs', there's definitely a jagged, ruined pile of debris leading down to the second level.

"It's a path," Malo agrees, and amid shocked yelps from the survivors below, we get moving.

Viera's ladder is a messy mix of shattered brick, twisted balcony railing, and torn things that, I'm confident, were worn not long ago by living, breathing,

Slaves.

The word sneaks into my head and stays there. None of those creatures came after us on their own, none of them controlled their arms and legs and tails or whatever they had. We killed them and it hadn't even been their choice to be there.

I pick from foothold to handhold, smoke and fizzy mist floating around me, and resolve never to let a Sevora in my mind again.

"I don't think we can pull the same trick a second time," Malo says as we assemble on the second level.

The piled debris block us from the platform, and there doesn't seem to be a stair in sight. But I realize we don't need one. Stretching up around us are strange, tree-like things; looping deep green trunks covered in bright pink flowers. Compared to a jungle tree, scaling one of these would be easy.

Down below, what Wem still in the dormitory are scattering, apparently the threat of death means more to the Sevora than it does to us.

"Just like home, Malo!" I shout, then take a step and leap through the air into a tree.

I catch myself one of the long thick branches, and immediately scramble down a limb of softer-than-wood material, placing one hand and foot after another towards the ground. I can't take time to look back up to tell if Viera and Malo are following, so I just move. Climb to the ground. Waiting for me when I step away from the ridged blue-green are a pair of gray-uniformed Flaum, who throw nervous looks at each other as I face them.

Yet they come towards me, holding nothing but their own claws.

"I'm not coming with you," I say to them.

"It's not your choice to make," the left one replies. "How you come with us *is*. Either unharmed, or otherwise."

I drop into a stance, extending my left knee and arm forward. Wait. They rush me at the same time, splitting themselves just slightly. I wonder why they don't use miners, and then assume all their weapons were blown to pieces with the actual guards.

I duck and weave around their swings. Flashback to games in the jungle, to exercises with Malo and the other Charre troops. I curl around one claw, slip under another. The swipes are slow, clumsy. These aren't soldiers, but I focus on evasion, on staying alive long enough to take advantage of some other chance that comes my way.

Shouts ring from behind me; Malo and Viera making my same journey down the tree, joining the fray. Malo grabs one of the Flaum from behind, wraps his arm around the creature's neck and then flips it over his back shoulder, throwing the creature to the ground. Viera has less luck, perhaps not as accustomed to hands and feet brawling as Malo.

So when the Lunare tries to do the same, she's not fast enough and the Flaum has time to react, pushes back from the Lunare, and moves to rake his claws across Viera's face. I interrupt with a kick to the center of the Flaum's back. One that sends the furry creature straight into Viera and knocks them both to the ground. Viera rolls as they fall, and pins the creature beneath her, delivering a pair of knockout blows when they settle on the floor.

Then we're running again. Out through the dormitory, into the hall. After decimating the guards and the two Flaum, nobody else seems to have an appetite for a fight. The hallway's empty, and at the far end, leading back towards the chamber where everyone had been yelling before, I see some species vanish. This time, I barely spare a glance for the swirling paints that, minutes ago, so enchanted me.

The great chamber is cavernous without anyone in it. As soon as we enter, the doors behind us slam shut. In fact all of them do except for one. The door where the Flaum force initially brought us in, the one leading out to the garden and the landing pads.

"Wonder which way they want us to go," Viera says.

"I suggest we take it," Malo says. "Every second here is more time for them to set a trap. Or worse."

"Then let's move," I say, and punctuate the remark by dashing towards the door.

Once again we're under the white-beige sky, running towards the giant garden. As we leave, our exit slides shut behind us. Locks us out of a place I never want to be again. Ahead, I see that the shuttle that took us here is gone, and so it's a plain blank stone courtyard leading to the garden. We run across it, not sparing a second for conversation. All our breath goes to our lungs, to our feet.

It occurs to me that we have nowhere to run to. Nowhere to hide, nor to go.

I wave at Viera and Malo to stop as soon as we get a little ways into the garden, when we're surrounded by strange looking plants that, now, seem more eerie. Their jagged edges and strange flowers loom over us, the ground under our feet is a prickly, sticky sort of soil.

A green fuzz instead of grass or leaves. A tilted rush of homesickness infiltrates my mind and I push it away, an act I'm getting better and better at as home becomes a place I'll never see again.

"I don't want to keep running without a plan," I say to my friends.

Viera and Malo, for their part, are holding up reasonably well. All of us have a few scratches, tears and cuts we received from the fighting or garden thorns, but we're standing, alive.

"Getting away from here seems like a pretty good plan," Viera offers.

"To where? Back to Nasiya?" I say. "Even if we knew how to get there, they won't be happy. We'd wind up back in that same prison, or worse. I'm sure they wouldn't mind sticking a Sevora in our heads either."

"Can we find the creature? The one that broke us out?" Malo says.

"Oh yeah, the one that dumped us right off to these monsters?" Viera replies. "You think it will do anything different the next time?"

"No, it had to give us up," I say. "At least it tried to rescue us. Give me a moment and I'll try to find its group in the Cache. I think they called it 'Dawn'?"

"This garden is not the place to do your digging," Viera says and glances up.

Not that I need the sight of the shuttle to tell me it's coming. There's plenty of whining, whooshing noise. Probably that same Flaum crew, returning to end our troubles.

So once again we take off running. Dashing through the plants for what seems like forever. What pursuit there is, we never see. We just go and go and go, and I lose track of where we are. The plants eventually give way to dark metal structures, to broad streets and thousands of eyes, most of whom watch us, their gaze pushing us down dark alleys and into corners where we think we can fight.

Where I hope we can be safe, though I know we aren't.

The only thing to do is take the Ooblot's offer. D'Rascale wants them to do nothing more than roam the casino's floor, looking imposing. Sax finds a flash of his teeth, a single raised claw is all that's needed to defuse most fights well before they start. Any that aren't convinced take a single whack of his tail to fall in line.

The monotony gives Sax time to turn over Evva's accusation. Time to decide what's gone wrong, to know who to trust, and he comes up with blanks., There's no real reason why, he thinks, the Amigga would turn on such a decorated Oratus. No real reason to brand her a traitor and want her dead.

Then again, she's escaped. Evva's on the run, which means she must have known this was coming. Is that why she told Sax and Bas to safeguard the humans? To not trust the Amigga?

There's only one certainty in all of this—Sax and Bas won't find anything on *Scrapper Station*, so they need a way off.

And one presents itself when Coorvin wanders into the casino. The Flaum looks notably heavier than when he was on *Cobalt*, and his scraggly gray fur is a more full silver. His eyes are brighter, and the Flaum doesn't shrink away when Sax notices he's there. Doesn't do anything more than smile when Sax clomps to tower over him.

"You're still here," Sax says by way of a greeting.

"Plake decided her crew could use a rest," Coorvin replies. "And she's still holding most of the food meant for *Cobalt*. She has to find a buyer, and there's going to be more options here than flying around at random."

"How close is she to finding one?"

Coorvin shakes his head. "I'm the new one on the crew. They don't tell me much, and, after so many cycles with the Amigga, I'm fine being left alone."

"Listen, Coorvin," Sax says. "We need a way off this station. To the Chorus, or one of the closer worlds."

"You're asking me to help you get closer to the Amigga?"

"I'm telling you," Sax hisses. "There are bigger concerns than your feelings here."

Coorvin, though, slants his eyes towards Sax, crosses his furry claws in front of his chest. "Sax, I'm not the one you want to be ordering around. I'm back in relatively polite society, and I'll be treated like it."

"I don't have time for that," Sax says. "How can we get passage on your ship?"

"There have to be easier options?"

"We don't have money," Sax replies. "Which means we need connections."

"So your plan is to try and get back on board the ship with the captain that sold you into this position in the first place?"

"My plan is to get that captain alone, and use my claws to convince her of the necessity of my position." Sax leans in close to Coorvin. "I saved you from that monster, Coorvin. All I'm asking now is an opening. Some information that will let Bas and I try to solve our problem."

At this last, Coorvin relents. "This is what I get for waning to throw a few chits on the tables. If you want to start a dialog, go to the

Junkyard's Rest—Agra-Red and a couple of the others like to go there after their shifts are over. Get them on your side, and maybe Plake will relent."

"Thank you," Sax replies, then straightens, walks away from Coorvin.

Wouldn't be smart to clue too many in on his relationship with the Flaum. *Scrapper Station* would have a lot of people interested in what the Oratus were doing, and Sax wants no part of their meddling.

He'll have enough blood on his claws already.

D'Rascale has them working opposite shifts, so that there's one Oratus present on the floor at all times. At first, the Ooblot thought he could confine Sax and Bas to their quarters when not working, but a sufficient show of Sax's teeth convinces the slime otherwise.

So it's not long before Sax gets his chance to investigate the Junkyard's Rest and the rest of the station.

Outside the casino is *Scrapper Station's* nexus—the large central ball around which the rest of the station spindles off of in various spokes. Cheaper to build a station like this and have it spin to generate some gravity than any other method. Even stations on the fringe of civilization, like this one, have some standards: every spoke is dominated by a particular type of purpose. From the Nexus, Sax counts seven of them, with two explicitly designated for living areas. Two more for docking bays and shipping.

Which leaves three for general commercial and entertainment, along with the space already used for the Nexus. The central ball consists of four main avenues that crisscross the structure, meeting up at various points. Sax walks towards the closest one, tracking the species he's seeing. Looking for the ones that might be disposed to a bit of chemical relaxation, and, thereby, interrogation.

That proves to be a difficult challenge—*Scrapper Station* is a far fling from the Amigga-run domains Sax is used to. Most of the people here, regardless of their species, look like they're clinging to life. Many wear motley rags, or patched together bits of garbage. Those who look nicer tend to display miners and other weapons out in the open. Sax didn't notice this in the casino, where automated scanners force everyone entering to disarm themselves.

It's a side of the galaxy Sax hasn't seen before.

But, despite the appearances, the species are stopping in the various stores, whether buying weapons, scrap, or any number of other goods. Including ones outside the bounds of legality, something Sax would have reacted to until the Amigga's power lost its hold on him.

That, Sax supposes, is the most glaring lesson of this dive into the rest of the galaxy. He's never held much love for the Amigga, for their distant and seemingly arbitrary demands, but he can understand working towards galactic peace. Some sort of prosperity. But this? This can't be the ideal. What the Oratus and Vincere are fighting for.

On his left, Sax passes by one of the large lifts to the residential spokes. Three separate elevators made to shuttle people up the spoke and out to the fringes, pulled by thick cables. A cluster of Teven gaggle together outside of them now, chattering about some sort of business deal. Sax doesn't care, moves on.

The first sign he has of Junkyard's Rest comes courtesy of a pair of Vyphen, looking haggard and tired, arguing about where to stop in for a sniff. Sax isn't familiar with the term, but among the list of locales, Sax hears the name he's looking for. At the same time, the Vyphen realize that he's listening.

"What're you standing there for, big guy?" the closer one asks him, a blueish creature with wilting yellow feathers. "We're not causing any trouble."

"I'm not here for you," Sax replies. "But I'm looking for the place you're speaking of. The Junkyard's Rest. Tell me where it is."

The two Vyphen look at each other, then the blue one turns back to him. "Up the third spoke. Ride it all the way to the end. It's the only place there."

Sax gives them a single nod, then moves on. He's seen the fear in their eyes, the tensing of their muscles.

It makes him smile.

Sax despises low gravity that increases the further he gets from the Nexus. The feeling that when he lifts a claw that it's not going to come down right away, that his leg will keep on rising until he puts forth effort to stop it. Even though the air is recycled and purified, Sax feels like he has to work harder to keep it down, to maneuver his body out of the lift and into the only possible option at the far end of the spoke.

The Junkyard's Rest.

The entrance is a wide, flat square that appears to have, at one point, been used as a freight exit. Too big for normal people, the bar has since filled it with glowing holograms displaying the prices of various specials and menu items.

None of which Sax is remotely interested in.

To help with navigation, all around this level and, Sax is sure, inside the bar as well, are posts coming up a little over a meter. He uses his claws to grab one and propel himself into the bar past a pair of nervous Flaum bouncers. As if they'd ever try and stop an Oratus.

Inside, Junkyard's Rest proves a slave to its name, and Sax wonders if its design has as much to do with the low cost of, well, scrap. Tables and chairs of every height are bolted to the floor and are made from random parts. Sax can see long benches carved from the wings of old fighters, while turtle stools for the fluid bodies of Whelk and Ooblots look like they've been made from rocket nacelles.

This all goes with the bar too—itself a long counter covered in polished scrap and serviced by robotic arms. Cameras project options down onto the tables, where patrons touch the hologram of what they want, and it's soon after flown to them by delivery drones.

Aside from conversations, the background is home to a low synthetic pulse beat, the sort of noise that doesn't cause unstable effects for some of the more sensitive species.

And then there's the Junkyard Rest's crowning achievement: a giant window along the very end of the spoke that looks out into the floating debris field around *Scrapper Station.* Lit by the reflection from the surrounding planet, the debris serves as endless entertainment as they bounce and clash with one another, occasionally interrupted by a passing ship.

What Sax doesn't see, though, is his target. Agra-Red isn't here, and Sax is drawing stares. He'll have to do something soon, or the wrong sort of attention is going to come his way.

So, for the first time in his life, Sax goes up to a bar.

Not a soul comes to serve him. Who would? He's a big, gray-scaled weapon that's still bearing plenty of scars from the burns on *Cobalt* and cuts from so many earlier battles that they all blend together to create a horrifying story.

It doesn't help that Sax keeps flashing his teeth at anyone who looks at him. There's a protocol to be followed here—namely, that prey should understand their place, and Sax considers everyone in here prey.

"You want something?" says a voice.

Sax looks for the source and doesn't see it, only row after row of bottles, box after box of stimulants, and plenty of inhalable packs.

"I'm using a speaker," the voice says, and then Sax sees the holes, right there in the countertop in front of him. "If you're going to order, use the menu in front of you. If you're not, I'd ask you to—" Sax manages to find the talker, a beefy Flaum behind the bar, who meets Sax's eyes and gulps hard. "To, uh, take as much time as you need."

Sax turns to the menu, a litany of options projected on the surface in front of him. Most of them are unappealing: injections meant to swim throughout a Whelk's body, targeted to stimulate and numb various nerve centers, coatings that, slipped down a Teven's central core, would drive the creature into oblivious ecstasy.

Sax scrolls through the options, writing off each one in turn. He's not here to distort his mind, the very idea of which nauseates him. At last he happens upon the very end of the list, populated with less dangerous things like water and nutrient goop. He picks both of those.

Behind him, Sax feels a stool begin to rise up out of the floor and, with his left leg, he kicks at the thing until its mechanical brain gets the idea that Sax has no desire to sit.

Then he resumes his observation. Still no sign of the Whelk, though Sax knows he's only been in the bar for a few minutes.

Those minutes stretch, and Sax orders one water after another, goes through several light meals of nutrient goop, and notices an ever-expanding clear area around him as patrons decide the potential danger of being near an Oratus isn't worth a close-up look.

Not that Sax minds.

He watches the junk spin in space, traces the trails of ships leaping in and out of the system. It's peaceful in its own way, and Sax starts to understand why people might prefer these sorts of places. A chance for meditative nothing in a crowded universe.

"You're not who I expected to find here," says a confused voice, one Sax recognizes.

His hunt is over.

Agra-Red stands looking at Sax, a straight line spread across his wide, crimson face, shadowed as ever by his helmet. The Whelk's embedded miner is still there, but Sax notices the battery pack powering it has disappeared—a seeming concession to the rules of the place. Behind the Whelk stands Engee, whose sticking a single eye out from the top of her carapace and turning it around.

"I'm here for you." Sax isn't a fan of subtlety.

"Really." Agra-Red sidles up to the bar next to Sax, then half-turns towards Engee. "Get whatever you want, I'm buying."

"You don't have to," Engee replies, but joins him at the bar anyway, sitting to his left.

"She modded my miner," Agra-Red says to Sax. "Boosted the power enough that it'll burn through even your scales."

Sax looks at himself. The scars. "Already had that happen enough times."

"You're still alive, so obviously not."

Agra-Red eyes the glass of water on the bar in front of Sax, laughs, then punches in an order for some drug Sax doesn't know.

"I need your ship," Sax says.

"It's not my ship." Agra-Red replies, turning to Engee. "You order anything yet?"

"Can I trust you not to leave me here?"

"I'll get you back. Provided this guy doesn't tear me apart."

"You're going to tear Agra-Red apart?" Engee pokes her eye-stalk around Agra-Red's slug body.

"Not yet," Sax replies.

"See? He's friendly." One of Engee's tiny arms shoots out from her carapace and slaps something on the bar in front of her.

"Friendly. You ever been called that, Oratus?" Agra-Red says, turning back to Sax.

"By my friends."

"Where are they?" Agra-Red does a show of looking around the bar. "Not here?"

"Working. The job you sold us into."

"Again, not my call. You're confusing me for Plake, Oratus. Take up your issues with the captain, not the crew."

Sax flares his nostrils. His long tongue sweeps the back of his teeth inside his mouth. Whelk make for terrible food—they're sticky, and they tend to fall apart into jelly after they're dead. Still, he wouldn't mind eating every last bit of this one.

But that wouldn't get Bas out of the casino. Wouldn't get them off of this station, to Evva.

"We need a ride, Agra. We'll pay for it."

"With what? Last I recall, you didn't have anything to pay with. That why you're drinking water?"

Sax blinks. Payment. He'd . . . never actually paid for anything in his life. Always on Vincere assignment, always covered by their contracts.

He has no way of buying all the food he's been eating.

"I know that look," Agra-Red says. "You're lost now. What're you going to do? Murder everyone in the bar when they come to collect the tab?"

"You'll pick it up for me," Sax says slow.

"And what would prompt me to be so generous?"

"You're buying her a drink for fixing your weapon," Sax says, then raises his foreclaws. "You're buying me a meal for letting you live."

Rather than looking scared, or threatened, Agra-Red jiggles his body and laughs.

"I'll give you this one, Oratus, you truly do believe you're frightening."

Sax feels his eyes narrow, but again Bas comes to his mind and he forces himself to relax.

"Yet," Agra-Red continues, the Whelk's eyes rolling towards a bowl of powder a robotic arm places in front of him. "If you really want a ride, there's something you could do to get yourself on Plake's good side."

"What?"

Agra-Red leans over the bowl, his mouth expanding to wrap around the lips of the entire thing, and, with a slurping sound, all of the powder flows up out of the bowl and into the Whelk.

"There's a restaurant, Nova. Residential spoke two. Plake has what they want, but they don't want to pay her what she needs to make for the trip to be worth it," Agra-Red says. "Make them change their minds, and I'll help you get your lift. We're going back Coreward after this anyway."

The Whelk is changing from his reddish hue to a purple color as the powder spreads through the thousands of spidery veins running along the slug's mass. Agra-Red's pupils dilate, his mouth goes slack, and Sax figures this deal is done.

He's never played the part of blackmailer before, but recently his life's been full of firsts.

Sax stands, and when the one bartender looks from his safe space on the far end, Sax points to Agra-Red with his left foreclaw. The meal debt is passed.

Sax turns, is about to make his way out of the restaurant, when curses, angry ones, billow from behind him.

He wouldn't have turned, wouldn't have bothered, except the panicked, slurred replies come from someone he knows.

Sax wheels around to see a pair of Vyphen standing over Engee, who, given her stumbling state, has taken hard to her drink of choice. A pair of other beverages, blue and green ones, now littering the ground at the foot of the bar tells all the story Sax needs.

Engee's alternating between apologizing and the kind of uncontrollable laughter that shows she's a long way from her normal self.

The Vyphen, though, don't seem interested. Their own elliptic eyes are bloodshot, and their feathered arms reach for the Teven, who falls over as she tries to back away.

Agra-Red, for his part, is slumped over on the bar, un-moving as his skin shifts between purples and reds.

There might be more than one way to get a ride on Plake's ship.

The Vyphens back away in a hurry when Sax moves to stand over Engee, who's tiny legs have her scrambling back beneath him.

"Have a problem with this one?" Sax hisses, low and with a single raised lip—just enough to show off his teeth.

The Vyphen, though, take the moment to recover and find some spine to stiffen. They both meet Sax's glare with their rubbery faces, their bulbous eyes angled right as the Oratus. Sax realizes they're the same pair from the Nexus, the ones that gave him the directions here. They're so divorced from reality, though, that Sax doesn't think they'd recognize themselves in a mirror.

"Nothin' you need caring about," says the right one, a blue-gold looking creature whose feathers are tight-trimmed. "She spilled our drinks, we're just looking for a bit of payback."

"Yeah," the left one, a mottled brown and green, whose own feathers are experimenting in a variety of angles, adds.

"Then I suggest you order your next round, and have her and her friend pay for it," Sax replies.

The Vyphen cock their heads at him. As if this is a ludicrous request.

"You're not hearing what we're saying," the blue-gold Vyphen says. "*Scrapper Station* isn't one of your military bases. We don't follow your laws. We're free to do as we like here, get what we're owed."

"Yeah," seconds the other one.

Sax unfurls all four claws, watches the Vyphen track those sharp tips. He bets they're imagining how painful they could be. Better make the consequences a little more clear.

"Thanks for letting me know," Sax says. "This Teven is mine. If you hurt her, then you'll owe me, and I'll take my debt the same way you're taking yours."

The Vyphen glance at each other. Then the blue-gold one puffs up his feathers, makes them stand on end like it's some sort of display. It's a rapid pop, and large enough that Sax doesn't see the second Vyphen pull a small miner from a holster hidden by his wild feathers.

The weapon comes out, aims towards Sax, and then the Vyphen simply disappears in a flash, a bright red one that leaves a molten pile of flesh and a cluster of falling, burning feathers.

Sax traces the blast back to the bar where Agra-Red is sitting, still looking droopy, but with his heavy, modified miner aiming towards where the Vyphen stood.

"She really gave it a boost!" Agra-Red laughs, then looks down at the weapon. "Added just enough reserve juice for a surprise shot too. Turned him right to slag. Excellent."

The blue-gold Vyphen dances a look between Sax and Agra-Red, then books it for the exit. Nobody bothers to follow.

Sax pads forward, sniffs and picks at the Vyphen's remnants, then grabs the small fallen miner. With his tail, he boosts Engee so that she's standing again.

"Miners aren't supposed to be fired inside!" the bartender's squeaking from his hiding space, but it's the kind of half-warning that nobody pays attention to.

The rest of the bar doesn't even seem to care—after a moment making sure they're not the target, Sax hears all the conversations come back, the music start playing again, and life return to normal.

A horde of small robots squeeze out of some vents and start dissembling the Vyphen's body, carting its pieces off to some recycler that'll, no doubt, turn it into some sort of food or energy.

Can't waste anything in space.

Especially opportunities.

"Did you not see what I just did?" Agra-Red replies when Sax offers up his defense of Engee for the ride. "I'm the one that took care of the problem. You're lucky I can handle my grotto snuff."

"I would have cut them apart."

"After that one had shot you with the miner? Cause I didn't see you doing it before. And they say Oratus are so frightening." Agra-Red turns back to the bar. "Get Nova to buy the goods, then we'll talk."

An impossibly dense array of lines and circles stretches out against black nothing in front of me. I focus, and I'm falling as the lines rush around. They expand and zoom in further and further, twisting into different and more specific shapes until they lock, with the corner I'm standing in holding center place. Then, with a little push from my mind, a bright blue line traces from where we are to an enormous oval that dwarfs my little hideaway.

"Kaishi, we've got to move," Viera's voice shakes the Cache's map away, and I blink back to the buildings and the thrum of ships flying overhead.

Leaving the Cache is always a disorienting experience, like waking from a deep sleep. It takes a minute for my body to regain control of itself, and I realize that I'm cold. I shouldn't be—I'm still wearing my mask, and Vimelia doesn't seem like a cold planet—but chills run through my veins nonetheless.

I've felt like this before, in Damantum, back when I had the high priest Jakkan's medallion around my neck. Back when everyone watched me, wondering who I was and why I had been so marked. No hiding then, and no hiding now.

"They're getting closer," Malo, leaning around the edge of the giant bin that we're crouched behind, says.

We scrambled from alcove to inset, ducking out of sight whenever someone started to notice us. Anyone here could work with the faction we'd just escaped, anyone could work for Nasiya. I have to keep checking the Cache to make sure we're staying on target. This bin—I don't actually know if it opens—is a giant rectangle jutting out from the side of a many-stories tall building with sides of sculpted, shining copper.

I suppose the reason it's back here, hidden from the street, is that the bin is a stark gray, mottled and marked only by the giant pipe coming into it from a port in the building's wall.

"Who's coming?" I ask.

"A pair of those slug creatures. They're wearing our enemy's colors," Malo states.

No worry, no concern, just straight fact.

Our enemies. I suppose that's what the Wem are now. Two major factions on this planet, according to Jel, and we've antagonized them both. I glance out the other way of the L, a way which ends in another short alley between the copper building and a neighboring, muddy brown tower.

"Then let's go," I say.

We form our line, with Viera in front, Malo in back and me in the middle. It's how we've been getting closer and closer to the spaceport, where the Cache is leading us. Assuming, of course, that we can even find a ship like the one that brought us here, and that we could find out how to fly it without Ignos in my head. A question we'll have to answer if we make it that far.

For now, having the hope is enough.

We go through the small alley, which curls to the right, back towards the main avenue. A place we try to spend as little time as possible. There's not that many people in the streets—most are in the tubes or the ships flying above, but there's so many windows and so much movement it's impossible to know when someone's noticed us. And, as the only humans on the planet, we're pretty noticeable.

"Did you find it?" Viera says as we head towards the main road.

"I always do," I reply.

"Are we closer?"

"Every time."

We reach the end and Viera freezes at the edge of the buildings. She's holding our only miner, which looks small in both her hands, but I can tell by the way her muscles tense that she's seen something she doesn't like. Malo immediately flattens himself against the wall behind me, getting his feet in position to spring, ready to dive towards the creatures pursuing us.

"They're everywhere," Viera says. "They've got one of those big ships floating there in the middle of the street. Flaum leaving in groups."

We can't fight them. We can't outrun them. There's only one other option.

"We need a distraction," I say.

"I can sacrifice myself," Malo volunteers. "I head out there, catch their attention. You two can run."

"No," I reply. "Nobody's sacrificing themselves here."

There's movement back from where we came. The sound carries on the slick stone ground. Slurping, squelching pops. Some language I don't know. But it gives me an idea nonetheless.

"How many?" I whisper to Malo and nod back the way we came.

"Only two, and inattentive," Malo says.

"Then there's our answer," I say. "Let's take them, and maybe we'll find something to use."

Nobody questions the plan. We retreat back down the ally, take a left and almost walk right into the two Whelk. One's a bright yellow, like Jel, and the other a putrid green. Neither is looking forward, both appear in some argument with one another. They turn just in time for Malo to smash his fist into the green one's face, for Viera, wielding the miner like a blunt object, to batter the yellow one. I, meanwhile, grab at the miners pasted to their skin. The weapons are partially inside the Whelks, as though sinking through their gelled exterior.

The Whelks take the hits, and actually begin to laugh. That's what I think the gurgling noises mean, anyway, given the wild expressions on their faces as Malo and Viera bring punches and kicks. Every hit shakes them, ripples through their jelly skin without leaving a mark.

I dig my nails and press my hand into the yellow one's skin, get my index finger on the miner's trigger. The Whelk realizes what I'm doing, and its short arms reach for me, but Viera grabs the thing's gooey wrists and forces the attack wide.

I pull the trigger and the miner fires, most of it still inside the creature. Its bright red laser melts the Whelk, turning its slimy body into a sizzling wreck. It's not what I'm expecting and I stumble back, my hands still holding the trigger, and I keep it together enough to point the miner at the second Whelk. The red bolts keep going, burn through the green one and cascade against the side of the copper building, leaving charred, broken bits sprinkling to the ground. Malo and Viera grab the Whelks' miners once I stop firing mine, and we're armed.

Which is good, because we can hear the pounding feet, the yells of coming reinforcements.

I'm about to run towards the main street, a tactic that's likely going to get us killed, when that bin catches my eye. The giant pipe running into the top of it has to lead somewhere—the bin's too small to hold something for a pipe almost as wide as I am tall.

I take my miner and shoot at the bin's side. The bolts hit the bin's walls, which break apart like paper. The superheated burns make a wide hole, and I find what I was hoping for.

Damantum had a rudimentary sewage system; a series of stone canals that wound below most of the buildings to the sea. Seems plausible here, in this improbably huge city, that they would need some way to move the waste from the host species. The Sevora, from what

I've seen, like things clean. I haven't seen a speck of trash anywhere, nor any of the usual smells of living things.

I smell those now. Horrible scents, burning my nose and making me cough, but they mingle with hope. Because there's a way down through the straight pipe. A way out.

"That's not where I want to go," Viera warns. "And if we get stuck down there, they'll catch us anyway."

"They'll catch us for certain if we stay up here," I say.

Malo brushes by me before I can head into the pipe, which is dark and wide, though there appears to be enough muck clinging to the walls that it won't be a difficult climb.

Even in our masks, the filth clings to our clothes, our hands and feet. There's little light, and the rays sneaking in through the hole above dim and vanish quickly. But we keep moving, because what other choice is there?

The pipe begins to curve, like a sloping J until it evens out going horizontal. Here the muck is deep enough that it comes up to my knees. We trudge along anyway.

"I haven't been this blind in a long time," Viera mutters. "Though I'm not sure I'd rather see what we're walking through."

"Does this remind you of the forest at night?" Malo asks me as we trudge.

"The forest is alive, it sings and cries," I say. "This, this is silent and dead."

Yet even as I say that, I know it's not true. Things shift in the muck. My skin feels the quiver, and I wonder if it's like back home. If there are strange insects burrowing deep, devouring what we leave behind. I blink my eyes, even though there's nothing for them to see, because such thoughts only distract me.

Far behind us, the noise of someone being brave enough to attempt a climb sounds. They're moving slow. Whoever's after us isn't all that thrilled at the path we've chosen.

Eventually the tube widens, until a much larger opening appears, and I see, courtesy of a few lines of low yellow lights casting their glows, that we've ventured into some kind of central chamber. Other tubes pour out, like ours, into this one, sending their sludge in slow spurting movements.

"One of the worst things I've ever seen," Viera says. "Here I thought we were in the land of greatness. Where miracles would be everywhere. And yet, I'm still surrounded by crap."

"This is the true nature of this world," Malo says.

"More importantly," I say. "We're alive. Now we just need to decide where to go."

We've made it to the edge of a large tube, one that descends too deep for me to see.

"Don't suggest that we climb down this big thing," Viera says, peering over the edge. "I can't see where it leads and I don't really want to."

"We've come this far. We'll keep going. Whatever it takes to get home," Malo replies.

"Do you have any emotion?" Viera fires back. "Do you think about whether you enjoy something or not? Whether you like the life you lead? Because I can't get a read out of you. You're just a statue that—"

"Viera, stop it," I interrupt. "Do you think here, of all places, is the time to have this conversation?"

Viera shrugs, but she does stop talking, which I count as a victory.

"I do agree with you though," I say. I join Viera at the edge and look down; it's a gulf, deep and dark. "I'd rather not make the jump."

No lights, except a small yellow trio around a single tube on the far side. One that, like ours, is gradually dispensing muck into its larger brethren.

"Do you think that's a sign? Do we go that way?" I point at the lights.

"If we follow those lights, the Sevora after us will take the obvious route too," Malo says. "But then, we don't really have another way to go, do we?"

"Not unless you want to take a dive down there." Viera nods towards the depths.

With our direction settled comes the hard part: how do we get over to the other side? There aren't ladders, handholds or anything else I could see that would serve to let us clamber around and across. We'll have to find something, and that's when I notice Malo holding his miner.

"Sometimes," Malo says. "You have to make your own way."

He raises the miner, leans out over the edge, and begins to stitch red bolts into the sludge covered side of the central pipe. Every shot from the miner carves a small ledge into the pipe's metal side; charring off the sludge and burning a line. The warrior holds the beams long enough to create a foot hold, then shifts, eventually going through all the power in both of his miners. By the time the weapons sputter to nothing, we have a semicircles worth of black jagged metal and charred chunks of crud waiting to test our weight.

Viera goes to take the first step and I grab her arm, pull her back.

"I'm the lightest," I say. "You should let me go first. The ledges are most likely to support me."

"And what if they don't?" Malo says. "You'll fall. Maybe die."

"If I don't we all will. For once, let me take the risk," I reply.

They look at me like I'm being stupid, but they don't understand how annoying it is to be held back. To be protected all the time. Besides, there's a chance that I'll find something on the other side to help them get across. It makes sense for me to go first. It makes sense for me to risk myself for the group.

The first ledge, a lip of curled, black metal, sits half a meter beneath where we stand. With Malo holding my right arm, I step onto it. I rock my foot into the notch, testing its strength. When it doesn't break apart, I step with my right leg. Plant both feet. The ledge holds, for the moment.

"Let go," I say to Malo, and he hesitates. "Do it, Malo."

My friend releases my wrist, his finger slide apart from mine and I'm free. That sensation alone almost sends me off the ledge, which is barely big enough for the front of my feet. I flex forward so that I fall against the outer wall of the large pipe. My hands dig into the sticky sludge, give me some traction even at the cost of knowing what my fingers are digging into.

"The next one is slightly up," Viera calls to me, as if I didn't know.

I take a look at the next ledge, and then count the rest. Eighteen burned-out cliffs carved by Malo's miner along the outside of the central tube's wall. Eighteen careful jumps to make; keeping my feet planted, my weight shifted. Any missteps would send me falling down into some infinite black. And, knowing what we've been walking in, I'm not sure I'd want to survive should I slip.

"Just go slow," Viera says, again giving the obvious tip.

I reach with my left arm and place it against the wall above the next ledge. No handholds, just muck. But it's better than sheer metal. I bend my legs against the ledge. I make the short hop, but as I do so I feel the first ledge beneath me break away, those charred bits crumbling down to the bottom. And as I land on this one, it too starts to bend and snap.

I have to move.

I flash back to the jungle, racing through the trees, and I move in the same way I used to when I was a child. I bound quickly, planting and jumping, oftentimes only getting one foot on the black charred edges. I hear Malo and Viera yelling, at first, and then they fall silent as they see me leap from one to the next. As they see me survive.

Left foot shove, right foot catch, my hands pushing off and steadying in equal measure. I don't even count, my every focus on the next jump. And then I'm landing, before I realize it, in the haloed tube on the opposite side.

I splash through a pile of muck and catch myself, kneeling in it, but breathing hard and too tired to care. Every single one of Malo's blasted platforms is gone. Every single one disintegrated into the depths.

"I'm never doing that again," I call back across to them.

"I'm with you," Viera replies from the other end.

Our voices echo around the tube and for a moment I wonder if we're giving ourselves away. But there hasn't been a sound from back behind us for a long time. Whatever's after us either gave up, or assumed we went a different way.

Speaking of, I turn and look into where I made my way. It looks just like where we came from. No equipment, no clear way to get Malo and Viera across. Even though I have miners, we're not going to try the ledges again. So I turn back to them and say I'm going on alone.

There's immediate protest. Malo warns about my safety, Viera, about theirs. About being left with nowhere to go. To which I say, "We have to find some way for you to get over here. Unless you can fly, I don't see another option."

I think we all know that, so after some more grumbling, the pair of them calm down. Take up their positions on the tube and settle in. While I turn to face the dark, and start walking. This is the first time I've been alone, truly alone in so long. Nothing in my head, no friends, or protectors. All that's here in this foul-smelling waste is me and the muck.

The soup in the bottom of the pipe sucks at my feet with every step. Every breath makes me want to choke on the heavy smells clinging to my throat. Bangs and rumbles echo around me, and the only light I have comes from those small globes, little points of white casting circles against the endless dark.

There's only one direction to go, so I trudge on. Think about Viera and Malo, trapped back on the edge. Any Sevora force finding them would have them trapped, and likely have them dead, or captured.

I surprise myself by laughing at the thought of Viera with a Sevora in her head. What sort of arguments she would get in, debates she'd have with the creature. Would she do the opposite of what it wanted just to spite the thing?

The sound of my own laughter rings loud through the tunnel,

and at first I'm fascinated. I've never been somewhere with a true echo, and this carries and carries.

Until something different comes back.

It's a grizzled grind, a shuffling of something large and stiff shoving aside the slop against the metal sides of the tube. And it's coming towards me.

My instincts tell me to run, to hide, but there's no place to do either. So instead I wait, hands clenched and defiant. The first thing I notice is a new glow. One that shines brighter, with long lights splashing across the walls in front of me. It moves, growing closer until it rounds a bend ahead and I'm hit with a blinding force of white.

My eyes try to shut, but I'm not fast enough. I step back without thinking and slip in the liquid and fall, splashing in the slime as the thing draws closer. The white blots out everything, and it grows and grows and I raise my hands to shield my eyes but still tendrils of bright squeeze through my fingers and stab holes in my vision. I might be saying something but I don't know because the growling, roaring churn of the monster is so loud as to render my ears useless.

It stops.

There's no rumble anymore, no grinding. Just the gentle lap of the muck around me as it roils with the settle of the Beast. The lights dim and narrow into a soft yellow, leaving iridescent halos in my vision, the same type I'd get for staring at Ignos for too long.

"What are you supposed to be?" the words have a leathery ring to them, like the splat of slick skin against itself, like instruments I once heard in the jungle, played by hitting sticks against covered, dried melon shells.

Yet it clearly says words and just as clearly says them in the same common language that all these creatures seem to use. My language.

"I don't know," I reply. "But I'm a human."

"Human? Haven't heard that name before. Admittedly, I haven't left these tunnels for more than a cycle now. Seems plausible the slugs above might have found one or two new species since then."

"Slugs above?" I try to pick myself up, but I'm still a little blinded, and as I rise my hand slips and I splash back into the mud.

"Here, little thing, let me help you. Stay still."

I'm alone, stuck in the slop, half-blind and terrified of the monster in front of me, but with no options, I do as the voice says. I stay still. There's a metallic whine and I feel, courtesy of dripping drops from above, something slides over my head, reaching behind me to settle into the soup. The noise begins again after a moment's pause and I feel first the liquid and then something hard press against my back and push me forward so that I'm sliding along the bottom of the tube. I yelp, ask what's happening but all I get is a soft laugh, a kind of willowy chortle.

"It won't hurt you. Just settle in."

My legs slide across the floor of the tube, and in a moment I'm underneath the front lights. The goop slides away as I'm shoved up a small ramp. The metal piece pushing me slams into place and I realize I'm not in the tube anymore. At least, not directly. Dim red lights spark up, and I know I'm in the belly of the monster.

All around me are scattered piles of junk. Or at least that's what I think they are, seeing as I'm not sure what any of it is. There's tangled ends of netting and string. Broken pipes and things that look like they may have been miners once in some distant existence but have now become rusted relics. While my first thought is that this place is immense, I find, as my eyes adjust, that it's rather small. Half as tall as the tube. Maybe four meters wide.

A swishing slither from above tells me I'm not alone.

"I'm coming down," the voice says, and, like on *Cobalt*, it's coming from speakers around me.

Something in the top opens, and a square of light—the same yellow that the rumbling monster shines from its lamps—projects on the floor and a moment later a creature plops down.

It's a strange thing, almost like a water droplet trying to hold its shape. A milky white skin, and two long stalks, that, towards their tops, form large dual-pupiled eyes. The creature, though, is tiny.

Maybe half as tall as I am. It stands, if you want to call it that, in the small space without a problem.

Then it moves towards me by shuffling its skin around and around. Like a jungle snake from back home, though this looks nothing like anything I've seen on Earth.

"Never eyed one like me before?" The creature says, and I confirm that it's the skin rippling together that's making the noises, waves crashing along its creamy surface.

"No," I say. "What are you?"

"Oh, well, I'm an Ooblot. You know, the things that usually travel in threes?"

I shake my head.

"Well, I suppose I don't know you. Seems reasonable you might not know me. But then, I have to ask, what are you doing down here?"

I tell the Ooblot my story. Spill it out because the Ooblot seems content to listen, and right now I'm desperate for a friend. Desperate to find some way to rescue Viera and Malo. This Ooblot might be my answer.

"Good thing you're not still hosted," The Ooblot says when I'm done. "The Beast would have picked that up, you know. These lights glow red for a reason. A specific frequency, makes a host eye's twitch. The Sevora can't stand it."

"And if I'd been hosted? What would you have done?"

"The Beast isn't just a junker. It's a burner too. I leave that latch closed, flip the switch, and then you fry."

"Then I'm glad I'm not hosted."

"Aren't we all. Then again, Clarity's Dawn wouldn't exist if we hadn't had our time with the slugs. Have to know your enemy before you can fight it, right?"

The name rings a bell. Ignos had warned me against it. But the other thing, the feathered, cloaked creature that had saved us from the first prison here had claimed to be part of Clarity's Dawn. So maybe they weren't all bad.

Also, the Ooblot claimed not to be hosted. That, right now, would have to be enough.

"I need to help my friends. They're stuck on the other side of that big cylinder behind us," I say as the Ooblot's eyes look over its junk trove. "Can you get them across?"

"Get them over the main channel? With this thing? How far can you jump?"

I shrug.

"Guess we'll find out."

The Ooblot rolls away from me, back underneath the square light where it dropped, and says, "Follow me right on up and we'll get to finding your friends."

The Ooblot quivers and then its entire body mass squelches down, expanding into a puddle with the two eye stalks, and then it *pulls* up and launches through the hole.

"Come on now, you can climb up here." The Ooblot's cheerful voice echoes from the upper level.

I blink once or twice, confirm that what I just saw is not some sort of illusion, then take some tentative steps. It's nice walking on metal again rather than the thick muck. I do notice, though, that what I thought was rust on the pieces of junk around me is instead dried dirt, the same mud from the tube. Seems like this Beast is meant to gather whatever the Ooblot happens to find down here.

"Do you have a name?" I call as I move towards the hole.

I stare up, again shielding my eyes against the bright light, and a pair of curious stalks appear, looking back at me.

"T'Oli," the Ooblot replies. "That's what you can call me."

"I'm Kaishi."

"What a cool name. Much better than mine. But then, we Ooblots aren't exactly known for creativity. If you want processes, though, we are your species."

The eye stalks vanish; T'Oli's waiting for me to come up there. I stand tall, reach up with my arms, and I barely get over the lip into the upper level with the tips of my fingers, one hand on the left and right sides of the square opening. There's no way I'll be able to pull myself up with my fingertips. I'm about to say so when I feel a soft, warm glove surround the fingers of my left hand. The glove suddenly hardens, locking my left hand in place.

I yelp, and immediately T'Oli comes blubbering back, its eye stalks showing again.

"Don't worry, that's just me. We Ooblots have what we like to call a certain finesse. An ability, we say. We can harden ourselves—as stiff as metal if we have to."

"You've trapped my hand?"

"It's hardly a trap if I'm willing to let you free whenever you ask. I thought having the grip might make it easier for you to get yourself up here."

I try, and while my left arm lifts me slightly, my right hand slips off the lip. "I don't think that works."

"Swing your right hand over here then," T'Oli says.

"Can you let go for a minute? I need to shift."

The seal around my hand softens and I slip free without an ounce of stickiness. I take a second to stare at my left hand, but it looks normal. No cuts or tears, no blotches or change in color. Looks like whatever the Ooblot's doing, it's not hurting me.

So I put both my hands on the left side of the opening, a little apart. Like climbing a tree. This time, T'Oli covers both of them and locks me in. I still don't have a great grip, but I'm able to pull myself up, high enough for my head get over the lip. But it's not enough—with my hands stuck and T'Oli in the way, I can't lean forward. My muscles are burning and in a second they're going to give out.

Before I can ask for help, T'Oli rolls forward, its upper body sliding over the hardened lower half. It rolls into my face and I close my eyes. I feel T'Oli transition to rock, the whole of it clinging to my shoulders, face and hair, and then the Ooblot starts to pull.

I wind up going up, then over the edge, facing down and resting on T'Oli's body the whole way. Until my entire chest is clear of the hole, and then T'Oli liquifies itself and slides out from under me, leaving me gasping for air against the hard floor.

"What was that?" I said after a few cautionary breaths.

"An Ooblot pivot," T'Oli states. "Turn myself into a lever and pull. Really not all that special. Do it all the time."

"Sure . . ." My voice trails away as I look around.

Where we are, on the second floor of the Beast, looks like the shuttle we took away from *Cobalt*. There are a few things that the Oratus called terminals; screens blinking with various diagrams and bars and numbers. Data that I'm sure I could understand if I had time to study it.

My eyes, though, are drawn to other things. For one, what's playing on the ceiling above me. Now that we're both out, a metal grate slides over the hole to the lower level and, as it does so, the light shining down dims and lines illuminate all across the ceiling; neon blues and purples, sketching out what's obviously a map. The dim light pulses gently now in the same red glow as the ones below.

"The map's my own design," T'Oli quivers. "Put her together based on what I've seen done in some of those paintings they have around here. You've seen them, right? The ones with the shifting walls? This one tracks our position, shows it on the ceiling. True, I can pull it up there in the screen, but that's no fun."

"I thought Ooblots weren't creative?"

"Get stuck in this thing long enough and anyone will get the urge to do something different."

I can't argue with that. Even though I've only been here a few minutes, the cramped ceilings and close walls are making me nervous. I'm a creature of free air—jungle forest or hillside plains. *Cobalt*, the shuttle, and all the narrow corridors on Vimelia do more to make me homesick than anything else.

"So where are we?"

"See that light? That's us. The lines are the tube system around here, and if you watch while we move, they'll change."

The mention of movement makes me remember that Vieira and

Malo have been on the edge of that cylinder for a while now. They might be in trouble even as we're standing here. T'Oli catches the panic on my face and, even as I start asking about my friends, slides over to the terminals and presses itself against the wall. All of the Ooblot sluices into cracks and crevices, hardens against levers and buttons that I don't even notice are there until T'Oli is grasping all of them.

"How?" I whisper.

"This is designed only for Ooblots. No Sevora Flaum can drive this thing, can hit everything at once. It'd take an army of the critters and this place isn't big enough for'em. Best way to ensure nobody steals it," T'Oli says.

"There are thieves down here?"

The thing's motor starts up and its metallic rumbling begins and then we're rocking forward.

"Some," T'Oli says. "Where Clarity's Dawn is those of us who escaped our hosts and want to do something about it, there's plenty who don't care; the injured, the ones no Sevora wants to keep? They get discarded. The worst, though, are the ones that want their masters back. That try to hurt us to prove they're still worth keeping."

"What do they eat and drink down here?"

"All depends on your standards," T'Oli replies. "The lower those get, the more options you have."

With most of its body immersed in the controls, the only part of T'Oli that's talking to me is two eye stalks and a small cream oval smashed against the central terminal. When T'Oli quivers, the voice it produces now is a much higher pitch than before.

I step up beside T'Oli, look out towards the tube. The Beast's bright lights are shining and guiding us. Now that I can actually see it, the tube's insides are steely gray and caked with what must've been seasons and seasons of muck and grime. Who knows when it's last been cleaned, or what disgusting things I'd been walking through.

I try to think of something else.

The Beast moves quick and before long we're back at the vast central cylinder. And there, across it, I see Malo standing watch while Vieira, curled as far up as she could to get out of the dirt, seemingly sleeps.

"Can you hear me?" I say.

A moment later a light blinks green on one of the terminals.

"Now they can," T'Oli chirps.

"Don't worry," I say, unsure of how to announce the fact that this giant machine monstrosity is not, in fact, an enemy. "It's me, Kaishi."

I can tell from the confused looks—Viera startles and almost falls into the muck—that they don't understand. So I try again.

"I'm inside this thing, it's like a moving building. Like the ships we were inside before."

"Are you okay?" Malo shouts back.

"Fine, and I found a friend. We're going to help you get over."

"Is it another Sevora?" Viera asks.

"No such thing, and I'll thank you not to call me that," T'Oli burbles.

There's a large *chunk* and the Beast emits the same metal whine it did when it pulled me in. Through the glass I see the metal grate that must've pushed me not long ago extending into the tube. It's wide and flat, and slotted with holes. Like the nets we use back home —big enough to catch what T'Oli wants without bringing the slime along.

The grate extends out meter after meter and then stops. There's another quick ding and the grate rotates until it becomes flat.

"We use this as a lift from time to time," T'Oli explains. "The thing is, Clarity's Dawn doesn't have a whole lot of machines, so we get the most out of what we have."

"It's too far," I say.

There's a good three meters from the edge of the grate to where Viera and Malo stand.

"I did say you'd have to jump," T'Oli replies.

"It can't go any farther!" I yell to Malo and Viera. "Do you think you can jump it?"

"No!" Viera yells back.

Malo, though, squats and stares. Straightens. "I think—"

There's a bright flash from behind them. Red, and it echoes along the tube until the light floods the main central chamber, then keeps on going past us. Rolling behind the light is a rumbling noise that sounds like thunder.

"Echo bomb," T'Oli says. "We gotta move. That light means the Sevora are bouncing sounds around here, trying to gauge what it hits. Guess you three are really valuable."

"Hurry!" I shout.

Malo says something to Viera that I can't hear. I lean forward and watch as Viera argues, sighs and shrugs. There's a bang as a second cascade of red comes through and both Malo and Viera turn their heads to look back on the tube. Viera's hands again grab at her waist for miners that aren't there.

"Just hold it steady," Malo yells our way.

Malo backs up, Viera kneels down, and, shaking her head, leans forward, gets her knees in the muck and presses her hands onto the hard tube floor at the very edge.

Malo runs. He clomps at first up towards the side of the tube, building up speed, then swings back to the middle—kicking up sprays of slop—and plants his left foot on Viera's back. Squats and leaps, flying forward towards the metal grate.

I catch the moment: one sprawling second of Malo, Charre warrior, floating through the air with hands windmilling, legs splaying as he flies towards the metal grate. My breath catches in my throat and comes out in a rush when Malo clangs against the edge and, his fingers gripping into the holes, pulls himself up. Malo lays there for a second before springing back to his feet.

"Your turn Viera," Malo says.

But she doesn't have the boost. There's no way.

"What are you doing?" I say.

"Being stupid," Viera calls back.

Now the light behind them is white. The same sort of running light that the Beast has. They're out of time.

Viera takes the steps, running hard, running fast, plants her foot at the edge of the tube, and it slips. She's jumping, but it's not far enough. Her hand stretches out and Malo slides to the edge of the grate and leans.

And catches Viera's wrist.

Malo's dangling there, holding on with his left hand. His feet— every toe slipped through the holes and holding— brace while his right hand reaches, scrabbles to pull Viera up.

Then the Sevora arrive.

10 / DEALS AND DANGER

If the Junkyard's Rest looks every bit the workmanlike bar, Nova fails in its attempt to be a restaurant of class.

Sax's experience with these places is limited—Vincere craft aren't known for their upscale dining options—but he doesn't have to look hard to see the many cracks in this operation.

Nova is nestled among a residential spoke, surrounded by the slim apartments every space station provides. Sax guesses, from the sizes and number of doorways, that this spoke is the lesser of the two *Scrapper Station* offers.

That opinion is seconded by the lighting, which strives for the bright blue of a healthy planet but settles for a hazy yellowed version instead, as if someone had released a cloud of mustard in the sky.

Nova announces itself by a spinning, bursting globe over its front doorway, a design that casts alternating white and sapphire-blue balls to the outer edges of its spiral.

The light show continues inside, where tables, chairs, food pits and other layouts meant for specific species dazzle Sax's eyes with their constant effects.

How could anything survive in here without going insane?

"Interested in grabbing a seat?" a young Flaum, looking entirely bored with everything, asks him as Sax walks into the place.

"Looking for the owner," Sax replies.

"She's in back," the Flaum says. "But if you're going in, you'll want one of these."

The Flaum points to a basket of what look like rubberized bandannas.

"Those are?"

"Easier if you just try one on," the Flaum, who's showing no signs of fear at the sight of Sax's clawed, scarred, monstrous self, tosses one of the black things at him.

Sax catches it with a claw. Stares at it. It looks just like a strip of clothing.

"You've got eyes, right?" the Flaum says. "Put it over them."

"Is this a trick?"

"Nah. It's part of the show. Twillo bought a whole container of these on a whim, which is why the restaurant looks so bad."

Sax hesitates, then figures that it's unlikely the restaurant would have some method of incapacitating an Oratus right at its entrance, waiting for him.

So he slips the bandanna on. The rubber seems to come alive as it slides onto his head, growing to match his dimensions and settling over his eyes.

Which changes everything.

Now the glaring lights aren't blinding, they're mesmerizing. They don't simply spin on the backs of tables and chairs, but seem to lift off and glide through the space, and when Sax takes a step, it's like he's walking through a world of stars.

"Pretty neat, right?" the Flaum says. "Bet this place would be doing better if Twillo could get people to put these on first."

"How?" is the only thing Sax can think to ask.

Beyond the floating stars, Sax can see streaking comets, the occasional bursts of light too—as if one of the stars happens to go supernova.

"Different spectrums, projections and mirrors, I think," the Flaum says. "Don't really know, but it's cool." She hesitates while Sax takes another long look around the space. "You, uh, still want to go find Twillo?"

Sax gives an absent nod. He might be a murderous weapon hell-bent on getting off this station, but he'll take a moment to appreciate something beautiful.

Nova's back is nothing like its front—trading enchantment and effects for the usual dirty gray drudgery of a space station kitchen. Species—mainly Flaum—run dishware and ovens, burning the solar energy the station gets from refracting mirrors on its hull. They spare Sax glances, and he gets some satisfaction from their twitches, but the staff otherwise holds to their duties with remarkable determination. He'll have to tell this to Twillo.

Or at least, that's his plan until he actually sees her, in a small office hiding beyond the kitchen.

"You've got a guest, Twillo," the Flaum announces, then vanishes.

Twillo, though, responds more like what Sax would expect. As soon as the door shunts open, as soon as Twillo catches sight of Sax, of what Sax is, she bursts upward, cups her limbs into her and launches towards the far corner, tiny wings flapping furiously. When she makes the corner, her four limbs spring back out, their sticky fingers spreading like webs against the corner's sides and locking her in place.

"Been a long time since I've seen a Quib," Sax hisses, then steps into the office.

He looks up at Twillo, whose round ball of a body is changing colors rapidly, trying, no doubt, to find the perfect shade of old metal gray to blend in.

"I can see you," Sax continues, then reaches up with his right foreclaw, almost touching Twillo, who presses herself back. "And I could touch you, if I wanted to."

The words have a deflating effect on Twillo, who stops her fluttering and shifts to a dull yellow color. As they slow down, her wings —solid, thin strips of flesh—settle against her sides like a layered blanket.

"I'm sorry," is the first thing Twillo says, her voice high-pitched and vibrating, coming from the small proboscis extending between her four tiny eyes. "The last time I saw an Oratus, they were tearing apart my home."

"It wasn't yours any longer." The Quib's home planet had been overrun by Sevora, and not all that long ago in galactic timescales.

Only a cycle had passed since the Oratus had cleansed every last life from that planet. That the Quib still existed at all was due to the ones that had been off-world at the time, and the ones the Amigga had grown afterward.

"You can't lose your home," Twillo replies. "I take it with me, wherever I go."

"Lovely," Sax says. "But I'm not here to talk about your home. There's a Vyphen, Plake, who's trying to sell you some food. I want you to buy it."

Twillo ruffles her wings. Keeps her limbs tight. "Why should I care what you think?"

"Because this claw can carve you into pieces before anyone could, even if they would, help?"

Twillo's four little eyes dart to Sax's upraised foreclaw.

"What does that matter? I have a restaurant on *Scrapper Station*, one of the worst places in the galaxy. Killing me would be doing me a favor."

"And the people that work for you? What would they do?"

"An Oratus appealing to compassion?" Twillo's laugh sounds like a monotone buzz.

"Then what can I appeal to? Why won't you buy the food?"

"Because I can't!" Twillo shoots back. "The Ooblots control this station, and they determine who I can buy from."

"They don't like Plake?"

"I don't know!" Twillo says. "They just told me I couldn't get anything from her, no matter how good it looks. Have you seen the nutrients she has? I think they were meant for an Amigga!"

Sax settles back against the door. Closes his eyes for a moment. He's well past his sleeping point for this shift, which means he'll be tired while Bas is off. And it doesn't look like he'll have an answer for her yet.

"There's nothing you can give me?" Sax says, and he hates the resignation in his voice.

"You want to go to the Ooblots, you'd better have something to offer," Twillo replies. "They don't give away anything for free. Anything."

Sax flexes his claws again. Ooblots are hard to kill, though. They have a nasty habit of turning to rocks as soon as they're threatened.

"I like your decorations," Sax hisses, then turns and leaves before Twillo can respond.

With his time almost up, Sax heads back to the casino, already knowing he'll need plenty of stimulant to get him through this shift.

Twillo's remarks, though, give him a plan. Next time he's off—after some necessary sleep—he'll march to wherever those Ooblots running the station have set themselves and figure out some way of getting them to buy Plake's food.

Sax hisses at the thought, causing a few species wandering past him to look over in alarm. There's too many webs here, too many connections. It should be straightforward—Sax provides a service, namely, not wiping Plake from the galaxy, and in return she gets to keep her life and receives a little payoff from either the Vincere or Evva, whomever they happen to find first.

Sax turns this over in his head until he reaches the casino, at which point all thoughts of Plake, her ship, or the Ooblots vanish.

The casino itself is packed. Species jam themselves into every cranny, some climbing on others, just trying to get a look towards the middle. Even so, Sax doesn't have much trouble pushing his way through—nobody wants to annoy something with this many claws.

Around the central bar, punctuated by plenty of broken bottles and sprays of powder, stand Bas facing off with D'Arscale and two of its Luto guards. Around them, scattered throughout the casino, are the ruins of a fight—broken furniture, sprays of blood and other things. The telltale burns of miners.

What Sax notices first, though, what narrows his eyes into a red-flint haze, is that Bas is bleeding. She's cut and beat up, and while her claws are still ready, held wide and sharp, it's clear she's tired, wary.

"Here he comes, to add to this disaster," D'Arscale announces as Sax pushes his way through. "Maybe you can get your pair to see reason."

"They attacked me first," Bas replies.

"Even so, slaughter will not be tolerated in my business," D'Arscale says, then the Ooblot swivels an eye stalk to take in the crowd. "Though perhaps this will serve as a lesson to everyone that my staff is not to be toyed with."

"This was an ambush," Bas hisses, her claws clenching. "They wanted me dead."

"Welcome to *Scrapper Station*—everyone's wanted dead by someone here," D'Arscale replies. "But we have to cling to the semblance of civilization anyway."

"Where are they?" Sax interrupts.

"Oh, your pair took care of them well enough. This station's down five residents today, all thanks to her."

Sax strides over next to Bas, they touch their noses for a second. He smells no fear on her, only exhaustion, and Sax takes a deep breath through his vents.

Calm.

"They want to imprison me for defending myself," Bas whispers. "Even though they came at me with knives, attacked my back, I'm the one who pays for it."

"I believe they paid for it well enough," D'Arscale gestures at several spatters of drying blood. "And you can bet repairing all this damage will cost me plenty too. I thought having Oratus would help me, would keep me safe, but you both attract more trouble than you're worth."

Imprisonment on *Scrapper Station* would lead to one of two things: being sold off the station for a profit to whomever wanted them, or being jettisoned out an airlock if a buyer couldn't be found.

Neither is an appealing option.

D'Arscale waits, with his Luto guards, while the murmuring crowd looks on.

The Oratus make their decision with a tap of their tails on each other.

To call what happens next a fight would be an insult to the word—Sax and Bas leap, together, at the Luto guards and before either can pull a weapon, both Oratus have their tails wrapped tight around the Luto heads, leaving no illusions about what would happen should their victims struggle. Luto might be rock, but smash them against each other and they'll break apart easy enough.

Eight claws and two slicing mouths turn towards D'Arscale, who reacts in the same way all Ooblot cowards do; by turning itself to near-solid stone.

"That will not save you," Sax hisses.

It would buy D'Arscale a bit of time—as long as it takes Sax to throw his Luto away, pick up the Ooblot with his tail and start smashing it against the ground.

"Then let's negotiate," D'Arscale replies, the flapping words coming from the tiny section of flesh it's left open for this purpose.

The Ooblot's voice is small, meek and pathetic.

"You threatened us," Bas replies. "Under Chorus rule, such an act gives us the right to eliminate you at our discretion."

"Though not discretely," Sax hisses.

"I get it, I get it," D'Arscale patters. "But what will that get you? More guards will be here soon, and will you fight the entire station? Even you both could not manage that, and if you could without dying, what would you get?"

"Freedom." Sax and Bas rasp the word together.

"Yes, until your own army comes to eliminate you. Until someone else here stabs you in the back, slices your scales while you sleep. Poisons your next meal. Nobody wants an Oratus in charge."

"Then what is your offer?" Bas asks.

"I'll let you go. Let you see my sisters, who can help you get what you really want."

There's a moment where Sax considers whether eliminating this Ooblot would really hurt their negotiations with its sisters, but the sheer helplessness of the creature is killing Sax's bloodthirsty drive.

"How do we know you'll keep your word?" Sax says.

"You've got an awful lot of witnesses."

Sax glances back at the crowd, and several dozen pairs of eyes stare back at him. To make sure they get the point, Sax gestures one claw towards them, edges out.

"You'll back us?" Sax asks.

His question is answered by a parade of nods.

"Then we have a deal," Bas says.

With the prospect of violence gone, the crowd dissipates fast, with some even returning to the tables and gambling machines, while D'Arscale's mix of robots and staff cleans up the mess.

"I'll take you myself," D'Arscale announces, thawing itself.

Sax and Bas release the Lutos, who stumble back, massage their necks and smooth their fur.

"You two useless goons can stay here," D'Arscale says to them before rotating its eyestalks towards the Oratus. "Follow me."

The Ooblot rolls itself out of the casino, Sax and Bas following. If one Oratus drew attention wandering the station, two of them with one of the Ooblots catches every stare in the place.

"We're celebrities," Bas jokes as they walk. "I've always wanted to be a star."

"How bad are you hurt?" Sax asks.

"I'll get through this," Bas hisses. "It'll take some time to get my perfect pink back, though."

"I don't care about that."

"Sometimes I wish you did," but Bas laughs, then, when D'Arscale sends a stalk to look, switches to a hard glare.

Sax, meanwhile, blinks. Appearance? Why should he care about that? Bas is a glorious killer who can wield words as well as her claws. The color or condition of her scales means so little . . .

Sax is still turning the remark over when they reach another bank of lifts in the middle of the Nexus. Only it's not multiple, just one large platform, with only one apparent option.

D'Arscale approaches the large glass gates, and they remain closed as it nears. Then, abruptly, another face appears, one that Sax recognizes:

The blue-gold Vyphen from the Junkyard's Rest.

"What did the sisters do to deserve the punishment of your visit, D'Arscale?" the Vyphen warbles.

Sax waits for recognition, but the reptilian shows none. It's a mystery that's solved a second later when Sax notices a camera's black nub above the door. The two Oratus are standing well back from D'Arscale—at the Ooblot's suggestion.

Now Sax knows why.

"Eneks, let me up. I don't need a reason to see my sisters," D'Arscale replies.

"But you have one."

The doors don't move.

"Are you really pushing me on this?" D'Arscale's injecting plenty of ire into its slapping speech.

"Yes." Eneks, for his part, doesn't seem to care.

"This would never happen on a Vincere ship," Bas whispers to Sax.

"Because we don't have any Ooblots to deal with," Sax replies, and Bas hisses a quiet laugh.

"It's about security. I need more for my casino, and for the station in general. Too many fights, too much killing. It's hurting business," D'Arscale says the whole thing in a rush.

Eneks finally changes his distant skepticism and manages a large sigh. "That, D'Arscale, might be the first thing you've ever said that I agree with. If that's what you're coming up to argue, I'll let you through."

A moment later, the glass doors slide apart and D'Arscale slithers through. As soon as the projection disappears, D'Arscale waves at the Oratus and they dash forward, diving through just as the glass doors slam shut behind them.

"What happens when we get up there and they see two Oratus?" Bas asks.

"I'm sure you'll be able to solve any problems." D'Arscale answers.

"Any solution's going to start with you." Sax settles into a crouch as the elevator begins to move, ready to spring as soon as the doors open.

Malo's still holding Viera by the wrist when the grate begins to move back towards us. It pulls along a pair of long metal bars that serve as runners and retract along with the grate. Malo looks like he's about to fall, and my white-knuckle grip on the terminals isn't helping him.

I turn around and dash back to the hole in the floor and ask T'Oli to open it. The Ooblot does so, the barrier shunting aside as it issues some command from the Beast's terminals. I slip down to the red-lit lower level, and look out as the grate comes closer. Malo's slid his shoulders forward, brought his right arm to double-grip Viera's wrist. Doesn't look like he has the leverage to pull her up, though.

Across the tube, a squad of armored Flaum crashes into view, their fur covered in patchwork armor and their hands holding miners. The first one points towards my friends, and the Flaum aim their weapons.

Malo and Viera are easy targets.

I have to change that.

I grab one of the pieces of junk, and throw it. It's heavier than it looks, but it flies over Malo and Viera as the grate pulls closer. The piece of scrap doesn't make it across the tube—falling through the air and into the pit. But what the junk does do, for one instant, is stop the charging Flaum. They watch the rusty miner to make sure it's not a risk. It buys Malo and Viera a moment.

"T'Oli, turn the grate!" I shout.

The Ooblot follows the order immediately, turning the flat platform up so it acts like a shield. A shield that exposes Viera directly to any fire.

"Now reverse," I continue. "Go backwards!"

The Beast rumbles to life and sprays muck everywhere as its treads take the machine back through the tube. With the grate retracting, and the Beast retreating, Malo's over the muck. He drops, landing in the goop with a splash. Viera follows a second later.

The Flaum, meanwhile, seem to be setting up on the other side of the large tube. Why aren't they shooting? Why aren't the Sevora gunning us down?

Oh that's right. They want us alive.

Malo and Viera run around the receding grate, dive into the Beast and join me. I barely have time to say hello before T'Oli's voice bursts over the speakers. "Looks like they brought bridging cables with them. We're in trouble."

"Can't you outrun them?" I ask.

"This thing isn't meant for racing," T'Oli replies.

"How slow is it?" Viera whispers to me. "They're all on foot."

"I didn't think it was *that* slow."

The three of us scramble up through the gate back to the second level, where we see why T'Oli's not confident in our escape: the Flaum brought more with them than just miners. They've launched a pair of thick ropes across the central tube, and each rope is deploying small fibers that stretch across the gap between the two cables, making a bridge.

But the real surprise comes when the Flaum start to run. They don't move like anything I've ever seen; each one twitches their feet and they lift half a meter off the ground. When they pump their legs, the Flaum burst forward, free of the muck.

"You've never seen mag boots before? These guys can move. No friction, all speed," T'Oli's burbling sounds awfully casual, considering the wave of death coming for us.

"How do we fight back?" Malo asks.

"We don't," T'Oli replies.

The Beast shudders to a stop and I'm about to ask what T'Oli's doing when it starts up again, only this time going forward. Back towards the central tube, back towards the Flaum.

Seeing the Beast come at them, the Flaum open up. Bright flashes of red and blue as miners unleash destructive energy against the front of the Beast. The bolts splash against bottom of the machine, and I can see little parts of the terminal start to shift yellow and red.

"How much can this thing take?" Viera says. "Because you're not really avoiding anything."

"She's a strong one. She'll take a hit or three," T'Oli says.

As we approach the central tube, the Flaum begin to back up and spread out, some retreating onto the bridge and others using those boots to push themselves up the sides of the tube around us. Their miners continue to unleash molten energy into the Beast, and I'm noticing new grinding sounds coming from its engine, but the Beast keeps on churning.

Right onto the cables.

"We're going to fall in, you moron!" Viera yells.

"That's the point." T'Oli's casual dismissal is the only thing keeping me from full-out panic—if the Ooblot, a self-professed member of an organization the Sevora hate, isn't worried, then why should I be?

And then the Beast's engine sputters to a halt.

We're most of the way onto the bridge cables, hanging out over the edge of the abyss. Yet the Flaum's ropes are holding, and we aren't falling.

"That's not good," T'Oli says as the engine whines down to nothing.

The Flaum notice too and hold their fire, start to ease in back across the bridge. I can only imagine the ones on the sides are looking for ways in.

"So what now? Surrender?" Malo says.

"We can't," I say. "I'd rather die than go back to the Sevora again. You think they'd give us any more chances to get away?"

"I need you all to run, when I say so, and push against the right side." T'Oli's command catches us.

"Run?" Viera's saying. "Clearly you've got the wrong idea about how big this place is."

"Do it! Now!"

It's the loudest I've heard T'Oli yell, its skin hammering out the words, and we jump to follow. All three of us rush to the blank metal wall on the right side of the Beast and push. At that same moment, there's a bang from the back of the Beast that shunts the machine forward a meter or so. Our weight, plus the burst, sends the Beast teetering to the side of the cables.

I see the world turn sideways out the front glass, the Flaum's mouths drop open, and then we're falling.

My stomach shoots up as my nerves freeze and my mouth opens into a scream. The lights outside vanish as we plummet, dropping us into darkness.

We land. At least, that's what T'Oli says. I'm battered, bruised and bloodied, having slammed against the floor and walls as we bounced off of the main tube on our way down. But in the end, we plunge deep into a huge pool of soupy liquid. The Beast itself doesn't float, and its crumpled body is slowly sinking down.

Muck leaks through the sides of the machine. Seeps onto terminals, drips from the ceiling, and even sprays Viera from a corner, coating her in brown awfulness.

"If we keep the swamp out for a bit," T'Oli says. "We'll be all right."

"We'll be all right?" Viera says, backing away from the sprays. "The fall didn't kill us, so now we're going to drown instead?"

"You asked for an escape. That's what I gave you," T'Oli replies. "Might be bumpy, but you're alive."

Malo lurches to his feet and catches my eye. We both move to a couple of leaks and press our hands, grab whatever's loose and push it against the creeping liquid. Trying to keep the Beast sealed for as long as we can.

"What happens now?" I ask T'Oli as we descend further and further into the dark.

"Wait and see. We either get lucky and someone's paying attention, or we don't, in which case it's been a real pleasure meeting all of you."

I'm sure my eyes are as wide as Viera's, who finally notices what Malo and I are doing and joins in our efforts to keep the sludge from completely filling the Beast.

"At least we'll die free," Malo says.

"I was hoping we wouldn't die at all," Viera replies. "Guess I'm the optimist here."

"Ignos takes everyone eventually," Malo adds. "Now might be our time."

"Would you all stop being so glum?" T'Oli interjects. "The only reason I drove off those cables is because it seems like the Sevora really want you. And if they want you, then Clarity's Dawn could probably use you too. So shut up, and keep that muck from making my poor junker too dirty."

T'Oli's words keep us quiet for a minute, until I point out an orange glow from beneath us. It rises up, past the Beast's splintering windshield and I see it's a circle, wide enough to be the entrance to another tube. As we pass, the orange lights flare and the door—a sequence of eight curling plates—slides open. The muck's too thick to see what's on the other side, though.

"Hold on to something," T'Oli advises.

There's a sudden burst of pressure and all of us are thrown

forward into what's left of the windshield, towards the suddenly open tube. I don't see it, but I can hear the door slide shut as the Beast passes through. What I do feel, what I do see, is the Beast slamming to the floor of a square room as the liquid sludge drains away through metal grates.

Hurting all over, I pick myself up. Look out at the deep red lights glowing in here, just as they did in the Beast's lower level. T'Oli said those lights give away if someone's hosted. Guess this would be the way to see if whomever owns this room had trapped anything they didn't want.

"This isn't exactly the front entrance, but we're walking into the only place on Vimelia we are allowed to be free," T'Oli says. "And please, please tell me that you're worth it. Because my baby's going to take a long time to run again. I don't think you appreciate the sheer horror of cleaning all the muck out of this thing's gears and grinders."

T'Oli's barely finished speaking, and I've barely finished figuring out whether any of my bones are broken—thankfully none—when a wide door at the far end slides open. It's big enough to admit something like the Beast, and it's lit with soft yellow lights. Another crew armed with miners comes out, only instead of the Sevora's endless Flaum squads, this is a motley mix up of species. Some I've seen, some I haven't.

"You get yourselves down and out of here. Sure they'll be wanting to talk to you." T'Oli punctuates its sentence by opening the grate again.

"Do you trust it?" Malo asks me before we move anywhere.

"I don't think we have a choice."

"At least this thing hasn't tried to kill or enslave us yet," Viera adds. "Though, somehow, I'm still hurting all over."

"I'd tell you to get use to it, but I bet you already are," I say.

"The day your warriors scooped me up from the jungle," Viera nods to Malo. "Was the last good day of my life."

· · ·

The three of us drop down and climb out of the Beast, with T'Oli turning the grate so that we can leave.

It feels wonderful to be walking outside of the muck for a change. My feet step freely, though nothing's changed about the smell. My mask is covered in gunk, Malo and Viera are much the same. We look more like swamp creatures than humans.

"So you found your way to us after all," says the watery voice of the lead figure, who I recognize as our would-be prison escape-artist even beneath his armor. "I wasn't sure you would ever get down. Jel isn't one to set people free. Not ones she can use."

"We had to work for that," Viera replies before I can. "May have left our mark on her home too."

At the creature's tone, the other five members of his team loosen their grips on their miners. I notice they don't relax entirely, and they're still spread out, giving themselves plenty of space should things turn sour. Trust doesn't come easy on Vimelia.

"The name's Rackt," the creature says. "Welcome to Clarity's Dawn."

Rackt takes us out of the room, while the rest of his crew follows behind. T'Oli announces it's staying to clean the Beast, and there's a lot of resignation in its pattering voice. Given the mess we're wearing, I don't envy the Ooblot.

Beyond the initial room—something Rackt refers to as an airlock —we pass into another tube, albeit one generally free of muck. That doesn't mean it's clean, though: junk litters the corridor, and the yellow light that looked so inviting from the outside dims and flickers along the ceiling as we walk. There's a sharp smell that burns my nose, a sour taste that lingers on my tongue and buzzes in my throat.

Malo and Viera, for their parts, keep quiet. I figure, like me, they're trying to take everything in.

Some part of me wishes Ignos—the creature, not the god—was still in my head. The Sevora could've told me more about Clarity's Dawn, whether to trust them or not, how the faction had begun, and where Rackt is taking us. Instead, I'm forced to ask Rackt, who falls back a step and walks beside me.

"The name tells our story," Rackt says. "A group of Sevora outcasts, left behind by their masters, came down here and found it to be better off working together than separate. Over time, enough like-minded species started what you see."

"And now you're fighting back?"

"Now we're trying to survive," Rackt says. "If the Sevora ever stop fighting the Vincere and the Amigga, they'd have the attention for us and we'd be wiped out. We're hiding in a bunch of tubes, human. We have nowhere to go, no way to get off this planet."

"So what do you want us for? You said, back at the prison, that saving us was a big cost for you."

Rackt pauses, gives me a straight look. "There are few known species that the Sevora can't dominate. Mine, the Vyphen, the Ooblots, who are rare, and, now, yours."

"And?"

"We can't let the Sevora tear you apart. They'll find a way." Rackt glances at his webbed, feathered hands. "That's why the Amigga pulled us from the war. Why the Oratus took our place."

"But the Oratus can be captured by Sevora," Malo says, now that we're all standing around Rackt and listening.

"Oratus are living weapons, bred and taught only to kill Sevora," Rackt replies. "Vyphen, we're different. Not as hardy, not as blind. The Amigga prefer species they can control, even if it comes at a cost."

Rackt gets moving again, but I don't let the conversation die.

"Which is it?" I press the Vyphen. "Did the Amigga get your species out of the fight because of the Sevora, or because of you?"

"You don't miss much, do you?"

"I've found my survival depends on it."

Rackt lets this go another few paces. Gives me a chance to get a better look at his feathers, which shimmer in the light. At first I think it's because the Vyphen are beautiful, but then I notice inconsistencies—patches where the gray and black feathers are dull. It's not the lighting, it's grease and grime. A glance back at the others confirms this—Clarity's Dawn isn't living in luxury.

Rackt did say they're trying to survive.

"We got tired," Rackt says finally. "All of the species did, not just us. Have you ever fought a war for generation upon generation? We'd get close to wiping out the Sevora only for them to appear, again, on some other world, with some other species subverted to their will. Eventually, the idea of peace started looking pretty good."

"But the Amigga didn't want that?"

"You're talking about the ruling species of the civilized galaxy. The Sevora won't submit to them, which means the Amigga aren't going to stop till they're annihilated. Now, with the Oratus, the Amigga just might manage it."

We reach the end of the corridor, where a wide set of doors trundle open at our approach. I look for a keypad, the same thing as on *Cobalt*, but all I see is a little black nodule towards the top of the circular door.

"Wave," Rackt mutters as we pass through, and makes a half-hearted gesture with his right hand towards the nodule.

I copy him, though I don't know why. A second later, I forget about it anyway.

The space holds a small underground city. A chamber that extends far back, down, and up. A platform leading to stairs sits in front of us, and, when I peer over the edge, I see row after row of bedraggled tenants, ramshackle dwellings made up of rusted bits of metal, shallow fires and even small sections where green things grow, with lamps glowing overhead. Species shuffle along makeshift avenues—places, it seems, that are clear only because nobody's dumped anything there yet.

But for all the grime, there's beauty here too. Many-colored lights are strung up between the larger dwellings, casting purples, reds and blues into the dim cavern. Laughter and the murmur of constant conversation bubbles up to us. The smells, too, mingle dirt and sweat with the meatier scents of cooking food. It reminds me of Damantum, of an urban life.

Our doorway is one of many. Haloed portals ring the chamber, some large and some small, all with stairs or ladders leading to them.

"Here we are, our home beneath the rock," Rackt says as we stare. "This is where the resistance lives. This is where the only free souls on Vimelia survive."

Rackt leads us to the stairs, which are far larger than the ones I'm used to. These are wide and long, and dotted with little beads. At first I think the bumps make them uncomfortable to step on, unlike the smooth steps in Damantum's temples, then I notice the mask around my feet grips to them. Useful, maybe, if I needed to run up and down.

"So tell me what your world is like," Rackt says as we descend.

The question sparks a waterfall. Words pour out of me, descriptions that turn into memories of my home village in the jungle, the desert plains, and the sprawling city of Damantum. Of family and sacrifice, of windswept mornings and nights deep beneath a forest canopy listening to the haunted calls of distant birds.

Rackt takes it all in as we go back and forth down the endless array of switchback stairs.

"You know how long it's been since most of these people have seen the sky?" Rackt says when I'm done. "Most, by far, were born here. Grown in Sevora vats only to live out their lives in in servitude until by chance or by neglect they managed to escape."

"I'm sorry," I reply. "I didn't mean to offend—"

"No, no," Rackt says and gestures with his feathers towards the mass of scrabbled shelters. "You should tell everyone what you just told me. Tell them that there's something better than being stuck at the bottom of a sewer. Tell them that their struggle can get them something new. Can find them something beautiful. Because right now all we have is anger. Frustration and rage."

"That only works for so long." I remember when the remnants of the Solare tribe attacked Malo's troop on our way to Damatum; they gave into their vengeance and were slaughtered for it.

"It's nothing to live by."

We reach the bottom, where I feel a thousand eyes on me as we move. The settlement isn't gridded like a city, and the paths that exist seem be formed at random. Junked hovels linger on either side of us, littered with species lying about, working or cooking or simply staring at us as we wander around various states of desperation.

From what T'Oli had been saying, I expected something more from Clarity's Dawn. I expected some sort of thriving society, an organized army. But this, this isn't even on the level of the worst Solare tribes.

Everyone here is falling apart.

I don't say this, not only because Rackt's fellows with their miners are still behind us, but because I know I could wind up in the same pen. I have nothing here, and the only reason I'm not dead is because I happen to be human. I'm exotic, a bargaining chip between species that want to use me.

We continue until we cross most of the settlement towards a giant shuttle wing. When we approach, I can see the wing's not alone. A few species linger around it and they look like they're chatting. What stops me, causes Malo to run into my back before he notices, is the creature in the center. The one that seems to be directing those around it with jerky waves of thin metal arms grafted to its body.

An Amigga.

It's not much like Dalachite, *Cobalt's* master – it hasn't spread itself throughout, linking veins to terminals. Rather, it's settled into what looks like a rusted metal chair. Those robotic arms look grafted onto its body, which is gray and patchy rather than the red and brown of *Cobalt's* master. Tufts of frail hair spurt from various parts. A single mechanical lens grafted onto its face twists and focuses on us as we approach.

"So you found them," the Amigga's voice, like Dalachite's, comes out of the vent in the bottom of the chair and sounds metallic, toneless.

"T'Oli did," Rackt replies. "By accident, it seems. They managed to find their way to the upper sewers, where they were trapped in the muck when T'Oli happened upon them."

"Our small band survives on luck, I'm glad to know it hasn't run out." The Amigga shifts to us. "You can call me Sapphrite. And you are?"

We introduce ourselves in turn, each of us cautious and suspicious. Sapphrite does nothing until we're done, when it gives us a slow stare.

"I'm not the first Amigga you've seen," Sapphrite says and I shake my head.

"The last one wanted to use us," I say. "Wanted to take us for parts. To make something else."

I'm not sure how Sapphrite could show surprise, but the zero reaction it does display only drives further daggers into my perception of the species. That the Amigga don't seem to regard operating on someone as evil tells me all I need to know.

"That should tell you why you are so important," Sapphrite replies. "It's been a long time since I've seen another world, since I've spoken with the Chorus, but the Amigga are always working on the next thing. The new thing. And nothing prompts discoveries like an injection of fresh genes."

"Well, that's creepy enough for me," Viera speaks loudly. "I'm sure you'll tell us all about what you want to do with our bodies, but I, for one, am covered in crap. I'm exhausted, starving, and in dire need of cleaning. So maybe this can wait? If you aren't going to kill us right now?"

"Yes, your needs are plainly evident. No need to fear, however. Now that you're here, you don't have to worry. Rackt, if you could show them to the Bunker?" Sapphrite says.

Strange, I don't feel tired. At least, not yet. All of the new things we're seeing, the people and creatures we're meeting, has me riding the same wave that kept me awake the very first night after Malo took me away from my village. But we're all dripping and dirty, and hunger, as if spurred by the idea, starts gnawing at me. It's been a long time since we had any real food, since the white room in Nasiya's tower up above.

Thinking of the Sevora leader turns me to Ignos. Is it still alive up there? Has it found another host?

"Kaishi, come on," Malo whispers.

Rackt leads us away from the wing but not back towards the tents. Instead, we head to a series of rooms built into the back side of the chamber, behind the wing. This space is cleaner, the globe lights here don't flicker much. A few species, older Flaum and Whelk, mainly, stare at us as we pass by, then turn to terminals.

"Most of Clarity's Dawn is made up of refugees," Rackt says as we move through the hallways. "Most have small skills, things like cooking or selling. Making supplies or other gear. There are other ones, like me, that have a more military background. That plan the raids."

"The raids?" I ask. "Like when you rescued us from the prison?"

"Exactly," Rackt says. "There's not that many of us, so we have to pick carefully. We need to understand exactly what we're doing, and get in and out before the Sevora can marshal their forces. All that planning happens here in the Bunker."

Rackt shows us to our quarters, a shared room for the three of us. The facilities aren't luxurious, but there's something of a shower, which dumps smelly water that's at least not brown. It feels incredible to clean myself off, to be refreshed. To remember every minute of existence isn't spent caked with dirt and grime. Isn't spent smelling of my own sweat and desperation.

After, there's a bowl in front of each of our small bed rolls. In the bowls are, for once, not nutrient goop but what looks like actual cooked food. I don't recognize any of it, but the collection of thick, colored petals seems plantlike, so I devour it anyway. It's sour, juicy, and one, a bright orange circle, packs a lot of tangy spice and I appreciate it. A little spark at the bottom of nowhere.

"The water's good," Malo says.

Each of us has a bottle, and when I try it I don't necessarily agree with Malo – the water itself is flavorless. It's been boiled, which means it's probably been through less than sanitary places. Then again, so was most of the water we drank in the jungle, and we didn't die there.

So I guzzle it down.

"When are they coming back for us?" Viera says as we finish, after each of us moves to our small beds, knowing nowhere else to go. "Because I am about to pass out right here."

"I can take first watch," Malo volunteers.

First watch? Here? Of course, these people may not be friends. We just met them, and Rackt made it clear we're meant to be used. Targets in their game. So I tell Malo to wake me up in a few hours—not that I know how he's going to track that time without stars or Ignos glowing overheard.

That question doesn't keep me up long: as soon as my head hits the pillow, I'm out.

There's so much green. It's not what Sax expects when the doors open, when they reveal a domed expanse with a view of starlit space. Soft grass splays out in front of them, broken up here and there with larger plants, and tables lined with the ladder-like structures Ooblots prefer to use as chairs.

A number of UV drones buzz through the area: floating bars that emit light and travel around making sure each and every plant gets the requisite amount before moving along.

Sax has seen things like this before—usually if the Vincere were called into some sort of celebratory experience as symbols of Amigga military might. Wealthy owners would point and cheer as Sax and his fellows marched out, and he'd look at all the worthless bags of meat and wish he could get back to his ship.

He feels the same way here. This isn't a place for him, for Bas. But at least there isn't a miner pointing in his face—the only one there to greet them is the blue-gold vyphen, Eneks, who looks less than thrilled to see two Oratus standing behind D'Arscale.

"I thought you said you needed more security," Eneks says, his eyes lingering on Sax.

It's clear the Vyphen recognizes him, but Sax isn't mentioning the bar.

"These two are the reason," D'Arscale replies. "They destroyed my casino."

"Self-defense," Bas hisses. "Your own clients destroyed your casino."

D'Arscale doesn't dignify that with a response, and after an awkward moment, Eneks leads them away from the lift and through the garden.

Beyond the flowers, there's even rows of growing produce. Vegetables and fruits. Sax bets that none of this ever makes it off this level to the rest of the station.

"Your sisters have a nice place," Sax says to D'Arscale. "Why do you have to stay in the casino?"

"I choose to."

Eneks burbles a laugh.

"We're not here to talk to you, Vyphen," D'Arscale says.

After the gardens, they come to a sprawling, if flat building. Too short for Sax and Bas to enter, the space is barely a meter tall. Enough, though, for an Ooblot to slide under and maybe enjoy. It's plenty wide, though. About a third of the level.

Then Sax catches what the roof is doing, and he's actually impressed. A translucent roof—giving those inside the building a perfect view of the stars overheard. Here, the Ooblot's home has the same, and Sax can follow the progress of the two sisters by the changing of the cream roof as shifts in and out of view.

Stuff like this is expensive, and *Scrapper Station* doesn't scream luxury. These Ooblots must be running some other game here to afford these things.

"I present to you, the Sisters," Eneks says a moment later, stepping to the side, keeping an eye on both of the Oratus.

D'Arscale closed his eyes for a long second, "You're gonna love them."

Malo wakes me some time later—in that dark room, I have no idea how long it's been, though judging by his sallow eyes and my own relative alertness, Malo held out a long time before nudging me. He mumbles something about no interruptions and collapses onto his own bed.

I blink for a minute in the dark. The last time I'd held a watch we'd been back on Earth, out in the open. There, at least, you could watch a fire burn or listen to the sounds of nature. Now I have only the omnipresent hum of machinery to hear and nothing at all to see.

Which leads me at first to my imagination, and then to the thing on my wrist. The dull emerald bracelet Ignos had given me. The Cache. It holds, theoretically, all the knowledge the Sevora put into it. I could search its archives and learn more about Vimelia, about the Sevora and, maybe, Clarity's Dawn.

The problem with the Cache, though, is using it is more like diving into an ocean than reading a page. I'd be immersed in its information, and unable to tell if someone decided to come into the room.

So no, I can't betray Malo and Viera.

Instead, I pace. Practice my silent steps, rolling my feet along the cool metal floor. I listen to Viera and Malo's soft breathing—and the latter's gentle snores. I run through the names, whispering them aloud, of all the people in my old tribe, wondering how many of them are still alive. How many of them remember me.

I wonder what my parents think happened to me—last I saw them, I told them I was going to stop the pair of Oratus that'd gone tearing through the jungle looking for me. When I didn't come back, did they assume I died out there?

Eventually, though, boredom rises again. There's been no sign of anything at the door, no message or word from Sapphrite, Rackt, or anyone. Anyway, they said we were safe here? That we would be their key to their plans?

That they wouldn't hurt us.

So I raise the Cache, look at it, and at my stare and with my focused thought it flashes in my eyes a brilliant green and I'm lost.

First I look for Vimelia, the Sevora, and I embrace their history of conflict. Discovery plays out around me—their first encounter with a crashed Flaum ship, the taking of hosts and slow growth off of their planet and into the wider galaxy. Even as these events play out, however, I catch one constant refrain overriding everything:

Fear.

I press the Cache on this. On how fear relates to the Sevora and scenarios swirl: fear of discovery before they as a species are ready, fear of losing a valued host, fear of their own weakness. And, too, fear of their own irrelevance.

For the Sevora, according to the Cache's records of thousands of debates, writings, and more from their own historians, have never been able to answer the question of why so many other species are self-sufficient while they are linked, inexorably, to the taking of others.

I rise back out of that despairing pit and instead try to find traces of Clarity's Dawn. When I do, one thing dominates all else:

Sapphrite, the Amigga.

The first and only Amigga ever captured by the Sevora, and done so early in their ongoing wars. The scattered bits about Sapphrite's capture reveal that, like Dalachite, Sapphrite had been found on a lonely outpost running all kinds of experiments.

I'm about to dive into the recording of Sapphrite's capture when my perception shakes. The Cache goes hazy. The words blur and then disappear entirely and I'm back in our room. Only now we're not alone.

Sapphrite is waiting for me to break out of the Cache, and it's by itself. Staring at me. The room remains dark, and, so far as a glance tells me, Malo and Viera are still asleep.

"Come with me," Sapphrite says.

There are any number of reasons I should say no to this, but the reason I agree, why I follow Sapphrite out of that room is that, to me, I'm still the Empress of the Charre. I still have a people, even if they're far across the stars, and those people deserve an Empress who tries all she can to keep them safe.

I can't do that by hiding in the room.

Sapphrite's chair goes slow, which I don't mind as it gives my eyes time to recover from the dark room. We wind through the Bunker's corridors and back out towards the wing table. There's nobody waiting for us, and Sapphrite keeps on going. Down into the tents.

"You have a Cache," Sapphrite states.

As the Amigga caught me using it, there doesn't seem to be a reason to lie, so I just nod. Sapphrite doesn't respond and I remember the Amigga, and it's facing forward now. Guiding us through the piles of refuse and sleeping bodies.

"Yes," I say. "The Sevora gave it to me."

"It is a dangerous tool," Sapphrite says. "I've known many who have lost themselves in one. Knowledge can be as intoxicating as any drug, and if you forget your body while you slide through a Cache's endless troves, they can be fatal."

I get that the Amigga's probably making conversation, but I'm not in the mood for pointless chatter.

"Where are we going?" I ask.

"Nowhere," Sapphrite replies. "I want you to take in this place, the species that are suffering here, waiting for hope, so that when we ask you, you'll say yes."

I'm not so cold that I don't see what Sapphrite's talking about;. For all the small cook fires, most of the species here look gaunt and tired. Sickly or old. Fur, when present, is patchy and the slug-like bodies of the Whelks bear a number of crusted, calcified patches.

"The Sevora could crush you whenever they wanted," I say. "It's not that they can't find you, it's that they don't care."

"Not enough," Sapphrite agrees. "We used to be stronger. We would hit the surface often, cause chaos. Try to get off a message to the Vincere with Vimelia's location. But we never succeeded, and now we've lost many, while the Sevora only get better at keeping their hosts contained."

"So what are you going to do?"

"If the Chorus learns about Vimelia, they'll send a force here too strong for the Sevora to survive. We need to get the location of this world out, Kaishi. You can help us do that."

"And what do we get? Malo, Viera and I?"

"You get to go home," Sapphrite says. "You get to forget about this world, this fight. Go back to the life you used to know."

I laugh. It's a cynical bark, but I can't help it. Forget? I would never, and I wouldn't want to.

"There's no going back once you've had a voice in your head," I reply. "Once you've seen and felt what we've seen and felt."

Sapphrite doesn't argue the point, but the Amigga does turn itself around. We're at the foot of another stair, and I realize there's no elevators in this chamber. None of the doors have ramps leading to them. The Amigga must have someone carry it, or else it's been stuck down here for a very long time.

"Perhaps not, but you can try." Sapphrite starts puttering back through the tents, and I have no choice but to follow.

If there's one thing I've learned since Malo took me away from my tribe, it's that charity is rare. Sapphrite's offering us a getaway, but it has to have a reason. Dalachite didn't care at all about anything other than itself and its experiments. I can't expect Sapphrite to be different.

"What's your reason?" I ask Sapphrite as we trundle by a trio of sleeping Flaum. "Why help all of these people?"

Sapphrite doesn't stop. Its metal arms hang limp at its sides as it rolls along. "The Sevora ruined everything I worked for. Destroyed my research, prevented me from completing my life's purpose. Bringing about their end by the force of my fellow Amigga would be the sweetest revenge."

"That's it? Revenge?"

Now the Amigga stops, rotates the chair so that it stares at me fully with its single eye. "I am going to die, Kaishi. On this planet, I cannot access the therapies that allow Amigga to continue on indefinitely. Riddles we solved ages ago are now coming back to tear apart my body. An Amigga may be killed, but dying? Of natural causes?"

It's expecting me to share in its bafflement, its head-shaking denial of a process that's taken every Solare and Charre for as long as humanity's existed.

"Amigga don't die?" I finally manage to ask.

"Not that way. Not unless you're cut off," Sapphrite hisses out a sigh through its speaker. "Which I have been, for far too long."

When we get back to the wing, Malo and Viera, along with Rackt and several others, are waiting for us. My friends don't look particularly thrilled as I approach with the Amigga, and I can guess why.

"Nice job keeping watch, Empress," Viera says to me as we near. "There's nothing I like better after a long sleep than waking up with this thing in my face."

She nods towards a purplish Whelk. The slug-like thing, for its part, does what I think is a shrug by quivering its body and rolling its eyes.

"It's my fault," Sapphrite takes over. "I asked her to come with me, so that she could learn, so that she can help you to understand why you'll be going back up to the surface."

"I know why we'll be heading back up," Viera replies, her spitfire returning with her energy. "To get off this place and head home. Right, Kaishi?"

Malo doesn't say anything, but by his straight look, I know he's wishing the same thing. Sapphrite, apparently done for the moment, only stares at me and waits.

"They want our help, Viera," I start. "And they're going to give us a chance to go home, yes."

"The way you're saying that makes it seem like there's a catch."

I didn't serve long as Empress—not before being removed by a pair of angry Oratus, anyway. In that time, though, I learned to recognize an audience. To understand I'm not really delivering a speech to one person when I answer a question, but to everyone.

"Clarity's Dawn needs help," I say. "They're going to lose this fight, and soon, unless we help them turn Vimelia into a target for the Vincere. Sapphrite has a plan, and part of that has us ending up with a ship and heading home, but we can't just leave on our own." Now I quirk a small smile at Viera. "Not least because none of us knows how to fly one of those ships."

There's a beat, then Viera throws a theatrical sigh out into the air. "Fine. What's this plan?"

"It's going to take some courage," Sapphrite says. "But I think you're the perfect trio to pull it off."

14 / ONE DEAL AFTER
ANOTHER

One violet, the color of approaching twilight, and the other a bluish white, like a new dawn. The Sisters emerge from their house like a pair of particularly smooth liquids, minus their eye stalks, which orient on the Oratus without surprise.

They both form up, standing, or rather, sitting at half a meter in height. Sax and Bas stare down at them, and Sax prepares to tell his story.

"Brother," the blue sister starts. "You've once again caused a problem. We've already removed you from this level, stripped you of administrative rights."

"What else can we do?" says the violet one.

"I have an idea, Sister," the blue one replies.

"What's that, sister?"

"These two, they are looking for our favor, yes?"

Four eyestalks rotate towards Sax and Bas, and the Oratus nod.

"Then here's my plan," the blue one says. "Kill our brother, and we will listen to your proposal."

"What?" D'Arscale flaps. "Kill me?"

"You've become a liability," the violet one says. "I agree with your plan. Oratus, do you agree as well?"

Sax looks at Bas, who bares her teeth. D'Arscale has done nothing to deserve their mercy, done nothing but deserve its own demise.

"We agree," Sax hisses.

D'Arscale tries to run, its liquid body squirming back while its eyestalks turn into that hard Ooblot cement.

Sax catches him with his tail, wraps it tight around D'Arscale. Looms over the Ooblot, then turns back to the Sisters. "How?"

"However you wish," the blue one says. "We're not monsters."

So Sax does it the kind way—asks for the nearest airlock. There's one on this level, ready for rapid escapes—so together the six of them cross the garden to it. Eneks places a feathered hand on the center of the circular door, which chimes an affirmative as it opens.

"This is what you want?" Bas asks as Sax grips the Ooblot with all four claws.

"Our brother has caused far too much annoyance to be left alive," the blue one says.

"It continues to forget our birthdays," the violet one adds. "Among many other insults. D'Arscale is simply not worthy of the Ooblot name."

"You're evil!" D'Arscale thaws itself long enough to patter out a series of harsher invectives, none of which seem to phase the Sisters in the slightest.

"Do you see?" says the blue one when D'Arscale at last falls quiet. "No use keeping such a thing around."

"Do it," the violet one says.

With that debate settled, Sax throws the struggling, helpless D'Arscale inside the airlock. Eneks shuts the door, and with a second press opens the portal to the cold void of space.

Sax is certain D'Arscale is screaming, but they hear no sound as the Ooblot is sucked away into the infinite nothing.

With that taken care of, Sax turns to face the Sisters and, at their prompting, tells them about Twillo, about needing Plake's cargo purchased so that Sax and Bas can secure a ride off the station.

"You don't like it here?" asks the blue one, who introduces itself as L'Reneo. "*Scrapper Station* isn't paradise to a pair of Oratus?"

"It's not built for us," Bas throws in a much more diplomatic answer than Sax would have managed.

"Like most of civilization, it would seem," the violet sister, N'Ollene says. "Yet we must continue anyway, even if our efforts displease the mighty Oratus."

"Your sarcasm isn't necessary," Sax hisses.

"Oh, but it is. We can't hurt you physically, so words must be our only weapons," N'Ollene replies.

"Why hurt us at all?" Bas says. "We want to leave, you can facilitate that. Do so, and you'll be thanked."

"By who?" L'Reneo says.

"The Vincere," Sax says. "They're looking for us."

The Sisters swivel their eye stalks towards each other. Hold the stare for a second, then swivel back towards the two Oratus. For his part, Eneks seems to be enjoying staring out that airlock after the disappearing bit of light that is D'Arscale's vacuum-frozen body.

"Then we can make a deal." L'Reneo quivers as it says this.

"I don't want any more deals," Sax hisses. "I'm tired of deals. Tired of wandering around this station and talking to people who are, somehow, connected to everyone else."

"Oh, but you'll like this deal," N'Ollene says. "It's right in your department. Your expertise, if you will."

"What?" Bas says.

"You want a way out, and we want a particular person removed." L'Reneo shifts its eye stalks towards Eneks. "Our friend's brother was recently killed in a horrible attack on this very station, by a Whelk. A red one."

"Kill the Whelk, and we'll let Twillo purchase your provisions." N'Ollene adds.

"But the Whelk works for Plake—if we kill him, she'll never give us her ship." Sax shakes his head.

"Then perhaps you'll just have to kill all of them and take her ship for yourself." L'Reneo says. "*Scrapper Station* demands justice for our slain resident, Oratus. Deliver it, and you'll get what you want."

15 / PLAYING THE GAME

I'm exploring the tents with Malo as a way to relax, to see and walk among the colored lights, sights, and sounds of species abuzz. I don't think the details of Sapphrite's plan have made it out to the public, but anyone could tell there's major movements going on—for one, the Bunker is flooding with people going in and out. The various airlocks leading away from the settlement open and shut constantly, as Clarity's Dawn agents, engineers, and runners send messages and materials to where they need to be.

Viera's off with Rackt, who's promised to find her some miners and make sure she knows how to shoot them. Malo's happier with the jagged blades they have scattered around—most seemingly broken off from scrap—so he takes on the role of my protector as we wander.

"In a lot of ways, this feels like my home," I say as we shift past a quartet of Teven huddled around a cook fire. "Everyone living, working together to survive."

"There was no existential threat back home," Malo replies. "All of these species know they could be dead in a moment if the Sevora above decided they were worth the effort."

"You don't think we felt the same way about the Charre? The Lunare? Either of you could have crushed us if you'd chose to."

Malo shakes his head. "We never had an interest in conquest. Plenty of land to the West for us. Raiding your tribes was more about keeping our soldiers ready, confident. About gathering honorable sacrifices."

"Well now I feel better."

We pass by a ramshackle shop that's glowing with blue light. I look inside and see racks and racks of small cubes against the walls, most of them pulsing. They're hypnotizing, and I step in, reach for one to see how it feels, when something long and furry grabs my arm.

"Unless you're pure energy, better not touch those," it's a rasping voice, quiet and harsh. "They'll burn right through your skin, melt your bones and turn you into a smoking puddle."

I follow the arm and see it's linked to a three-limbed, monstrous thing with what looks like a half-mouth sticking up and out of a wide torso. As if a Flaum and Amigga had been smashed together, without much care for how things fit.

"Keep your hands off her," Malo says, stepping between us.

"Meant no harm," the creature's mouth twists and snaps as it talks. "Just trying to keep your friend from killing herself."

"Thank you," I speak quickly. "For the warning."

I don't see any eyes on the creature, yet it clearly knows where we stand, as it's oriented towards us, and its central arm—the one that grabbed me—hangs ready to reach out again. The other two limbs, its legs, end in what appear to be massive, but thin feet.

"What are you?" Malo asks the question, which I'm thankful for, even if it comes off as rude.

"An accident." The creature doesn't seem the slightest bit embarrassed about this. "A Sevora mistake. An old one, too. Tried coupling different species in one of their vats, and when it didn't work out, they tried to have me killed."

"You escaped?"

"Freed," the creature scrapes a laugh. "The Sevora scientist that grew me thought it'd be cruel to burn me down. So it let me go in the sewers instead, like that's some kind of mercy. Fell my way down here and look, a useless split-breed keeping watch on batteries. What an achievement."

"So these go in the miners?" I nod towards the cubes.

"Everything else too," the creature replies. "We siphon off what power we can from up above. It's not much, but it keeps this place warm, the filters running and our weapons with enough juice to cause some damage."

"You don't seem that excited?"

"What's there to be excited about? That attack Sapphrite's planning?" Again the creature falls into its hacking laugh, which is starting to annoy me. "We've done hundreds of those. They cause some chaos, but the Sevora always drive us away. Then they come for revenge, but their factions keep anyone from committing too much, so we nurse our wounds and wait to try again."

"You can't win a war that way." Malo glances at me, his eyes moving towards the exit. "There has to be drive, a willingness to keep fighting until the enemy is gone."

"Or you've made peace," I add, taking my own step away from the creature.

"Peace. There's a funny idea. You think I'm down here because I declared war on the Sevora?" The creature follows us as we step away from the glowing cubes. "No. They wanted me gone because I reminded them of their own failures. I'm a stain to be wiped away, not something to be bargained with."

We reach the edge of the shop and keep going, both of us making half-hearted goodbyes.

"To them, we're nothing!" the creature calls as we head away. "Nothing!"

We make it to a quiet spot with a few scattered boxes between a pair of larger tents. A string of glowing green lights gives the clearing a calming ambiance, which is what I'm looking for after the encounter with the strange battery keeper.

"Looks like the jungle, doesn't it?" I say to Malo as I head for the box.

It's not exactly a comfortable chair, but just sitting for a moment gives my mind a chance to reset. To breath in the smells and wind them around thoughts. So many of them on the edge of familiarity, so many entirely new.

"I don't know what jungle you lived in, Kaishi, but the one I remember didn't have lights like these." Malo sits down near me. I notice he's picked up a broken bar of metal from somewhere and holds it like he used to hold his spear.

"It hasn't been all that long," I say. "But it feels like forever since we've left home."

"The flow of time is driven less by the passing of days and more by experiences," Malo replies. "At least, that's what our warriors would tell novices when we trained. Their point, I think, is that we would forget the hours in their monotonous lessons and remember the results."

"Did you?"

"I'm still alive, so I suppose so."

I nod towards the metal stick. "And you've remembered to always keep a weapon handy."

"I don't need to remember that, Empress," Malo looks at the staff as if it's the most valuable thing he owns. "These adventures have taught me that every moment I'm without one, I'm vulnerable."

"You're a good soldier, Malo," I say, and throw him a smile to take the edge off what I say next. "But you could be a better friend."

"A better friend?"

"You're so serious. Always about the mission, keeping me alive, or watching for the next threat. Not every danger comes from the outside, you know."

"Are you okay, Kaishi?"

"Look, Malo, let's not ask about me for a change. What about you? Are you okay?"

This question seems to have Malo confused. "I'm fine, Empress."

"No, that's not what I'm asking. How do you feel about everything we've been through? About what Sapphrite's asking us to do?"

Now he gets it. Takes his eyes from mine and sweeps them along parts of the settlement we can see.

"There's nothing I've lived that could have prepared me for this," Malo starts. "It's one surprise after another, which I'm able to handle. What's harder, though, is seeing all of the constructs I've lived with torn away. I once thought the Charre were the best people alive, and now I know we're nothing next to all of these others. If they wanted to, the Sevora could destroy us. So could the Vincere. I have no doubt that Clarity's Dawn, bedraggled and lost as they are, would make a mockery of all our warriors and their years of wielding spears and shooting arrows. In short, Kaishi, I feel pointless."

In Malo's words I hear my own thoughts crystallized—we, humanity, are being reduced to bargaining chips by races far stronger than our own. We'd gone from masters of our own destinies to pawns in a game I can barely conceive, much less play.

But then, here we are, immersed in a band full of rebels, refugees, and refuse who won't accept that their role is one of servitude, that their destiny is decided by others.

"We have to take it back," I whisper the words at first. "Our agency, our choice."

"How?"

"We start here. With Sapphrite's plan. We start by speaking up. You've led a hundred raids. I've been sneaking around jungles since I could walk. And Viera . . ."

"Viera's unpredictable, but always in our favor," Malo finishes for me.

"Exactly. This might be the home of Clarity's Dawn, and this might be their idea, but if we're going to carry it out, then humans are going to have a stake in it."

Just saying the words helps. My blood pumps harder, my smile feels more confident than it has been at any point since we've left Damantum.

Malo grabs my left hand hard. It's been a long time since I've felt his grip, warm and rough. There's a lot packed into his touch, and I meet his look not as Empress, not as a Solare chief's daughter, but as a friend finding strength in another.

16 / INTERRUPTED NEGOTIATIONS

Once again, Sax finds himself wishing for the simple clarity of a Vincere mission. A commander, an objective, and a horde of evil Sevora to destroy. Instead, he and Bas set off down the lift, back to the station proper, in search of Agra-Red. Though what he'll do when Sax finds the Whelk is a question he can't answer.

Back in the Nexus, Sax takes a step out of the lift, looking for the way to the docking spoke, when Bas taps his shoulder with her right foreclaw.

"Sax, before we go on, I need to take care of . . . myself." Bas looks down at the cuts and gashes, her bent scales.

As if the act of recognizing they're living, breathing creatures breaks a spell, Sax feels his own crushing exhaustion weighing in. They need a place to sleep, they need medical supplies. And neither can be had for free. Still, they first go to the only infirmary on the station, a place labeled only by a glowing bright green circle—that universal sign of health.

Inside, a pair of cheery Teven tell Sax and Bas that the cost of treatment by the medical robots, and staying in one of the recovery rooms, will run far more than either Oratus has to give.

Sax is ready to return to the tried-and-true flashing of his claws, but Bas stops him with a tap of her tail.

"We don't have payment," Bas says. "But we do have influence."

"What kind of influence?" the lead Teven, one with an unusual striping black and purple carapace, replies. "We don't need more space, and the Sisters would never replace us."

"With your customers," Bas hisses, and she looks at her claws. "We'll bring you more, plenty more, if you fix us now."

The Teven, their eyes peeking through the holes in their long shells, stare at the claws, then so a short dance with their limbs beating on each other's shells.

Sax always hates secret languages.

"How many fights are you planning to start?" the lead Teven says.

"Many," Sax replies.

"Hopefully not enough to take apart the station?"

"No." Sax has no idea what it would take to destroy *Scrapper Station*, but he's reasonably confident things won't come to that.

Though Sax and Bas have left their fair share of wreckage behind, *Cobalt* included.

"Then, if you can guarantee at least five other customers, I'll waive your repair and rest fees."

It's a deal. The Teven don't have Oratus-specific care rooms—there are so few of the species outside of the Vincere that it wouldn't make sense—so Sax and Bas separate. Each of them take one of the largest rooms available, normally meant for heavy Whelk.

The rooms themselves are clear, cream. Tiled across the floors and walls. Sax isn't sure why until hoses blast him with water from all sides. Only it's not just water—the stuff clings to him, seems to squirm across his scales.

Nanobots.

The little things nip and bite, knit and sew Sax's body back together. Sax doesn't think he has many new injuries, but then he feels his legs tickle, tear, and grow.

They're repairing the burns, grafting and splicing new skin and scales right there.

Well before the nanobots are done, Sax is ushered out to a recovery room, a tranquil, silent box looking out into space and the stars. Again, no Oratus chairs here, but Sax makes do with a large couch. A serving robot hovers over with nutrient drink, and Sax takes a long sip, feels the nanobots whir away, and drifts into a long-sought sleep.

The *Mobius* waits for them in Docking Spoke One. Sax feels better than he has in a long time—though the Teven remind them when they leave of their promised 'referrals'.

Not that Sax cares—if they don't have to carve up a half-dozen people, then he's fine keeping his claws put away. The Teven can't exactly do much to enforce their end of the deal.

Docked, the *Mobius* looks like it belongs here. Every part of the ship seems to be meant for something else. The outside is a dozen different colors, all of them pitted and scarred from space debris. Engines, weapons, and living modules spring off the large cargo core at various angles, such that Sax thinks Plake must give her crew freedom to do what they like to her ship.

"It'll never win a fight in heavy atmosphere," Coorvin says, stepping down from the ship's ramp towards them. "Plake, though, says she belongs in deep space. Doesn't ever want to take this thing to another Amigga planet."

The little old Flaum steps over, looks at each of them.

"Did D'Arscale send you here?" Coorvin finally asks.

Sax decides the Flaum doesn't deserve to be sent to the Teven.

"D'Arscale is enjoying a scenic tour of local space," Bas grins wide. Her rose-gold scales glitter in the bright docking bay light, shined enough by their recent repair that Coorvin even winces a little.

"Ah," the Flaum replies. "So this is . . . a social call?"

"Have you heard of the Sisters?" Sax asks, and when Coorvin shakes his head, Sax fills the Flaum in.

"Plake's not going to be happy if you kill Agra-Red," Coorvin glances behind him, back up the ramp. "The Whelk's been her muscle for a long time."

"Which is why we're standing here, in the open," Bas says. "We want a lift off of the station. Plake has a chance, now, to give us that, either with Agra-Red or without him."

"Why don't you try one of the other ships?" Coorvin nods behind them. "There's at least a dozen more docked."

If Sax has to explain all the twisting events that led to them being here, one more time, he's going to start murdering everything in sight.

"We have no money," Sax leaves his summary short. "We need leverage with anyone who will take us. The Sisters give us that leverage."

"I think you'll find the Sisters won't give you as much as you need," Coorvin says. "But I'll get Plake and you can make your case to her."

The Flaum vanishes back up the ramp.

"If they attack us," Sax says. "I'll take the Whelk."

"Trying to protect me?" Bas replies.

Sax hisses a laugh, "I think Whelk are tasty."

They're not waiting long till Coorvin reappears, with Plake in tow. The Vyphen's not looking thrilled to see them, though her expression changes, as does all of them, when the space station's alarms begin to go off.

"Vincere vessel approaching!" announces a voice that Sax recognizes as Eneks. "Anyone that wants to run, your time is now. *Scrapper Station* accepts no liability for any consequences of your attempted escape!"

"Guess that means you should run," Sax says to Plake, who laughs.

"Why? You going to try and get revenge? I was just selling my cargo for a good price."

"You sold us into slavery."

"Hardly," Plake's rubbery mouth slides into a frown. "D'Arscale said you'd eventually be released to the Vincere, that he'd take any blame for keeping you."

"D'Arscale is an icicle now," Bas replies. "Which means—"

Plake waves her feathered arm. "Stop. I don't take threats from Oratus. Your way out is here. Take it. You can try to implicate me if you want, but I saved your damn lives. Feel like that's worth an even trade for mine and my crew. You Oratus are all about honor, right?"

Sax feels the Oratus are more about highly efficient slaughter, but honor works.

"We'll let you go," Sax acknowledges, and together the two Oratus turn to leave the twisting mess of demands from the Sisters, from Plake and Twillo behind.

Guess the Teven definitely won't be getting their payback now.

The docking spoke clears rapidly after the Vincere arrival is announced. Ships scatter off the station, leaping away to anywhere other than here, anywhere they won't be trapped and inspected and, without doubt or mercy, eviscerated.

What fascinates Sax, though, is that the Vincere vessel, a light frigate with plenty of fighter support, doesn't make any moves against the smugglers. Doesn't make any attempts to enforce the police action that is the reason for its existence. All it does is stay near the station and launch a single shuttle, an oval-shaped, unarmed transport craft that floats over to Scrapper Station.

Sax and Bas watch the entire thing play out on one of the several giant displays within the Docking Spoke that show everything happening around the station. Ships are represented as little diamonds, the points showing their headings, while the frigate is designated as a big red circle. The red, according to a wide legend on the right, a glaring reminder of its likely hostility.

The shuttle shows as a bright blue diamond—a harmless designation—and, as it nears the station, a number six appears inside its shape.

"Betting that's our ride," Bas says and Sax agrees, so they head to bay six and wait.

The shuttle lands shortly after, tall struts untangling themselves from the base of the craft and, with magnetic jets burning silent, the shuttle settles onto the bay floor. Rather than a ramp, a platform descends from the craft's center, plenty wide for four Oratus, though this one only holds two.

Ones Bas and Sax recognize: Gar and Lan.

And they're ready for war; loaded with miners, wearing masks, and casting their heads about for trouble. When they center on Sax and Bas, Gar looks disappointed.

"Guess we scared away all the prey?" Gar says as the two Oratus bound over.

"There's plenty back in the station, if you're hungry." Sax shrugs.

"That's the not mission," Lan says.

"It never is." Gar looks mournfully at his claws.

"What is the mission?" Bas asks.

"You."

I resist reaching for my scalp, scratching at it. Drawing attention to what's there. The ride, though, is boring—a slow crawl up the tubes towards the surface in a mostly-fixed Beast.

T'Oli is back at the controls, its hard-white form navigating the Beast around bumps and ridges as we scale the walls. The machine's treads bite into the tube's sides and allow it to climb. To bring us closer to death.

Malo and Viera sit next to me, strapped into a trio of hard slats that explore new dimensions of discomfort by pressing into seemingly every nook of my back at once.

"Made for Ooblots," T'Oli said when we climbed in. "We fit everything, so everything fits us."

So to keep myself from going insane at the pinching, I think about how, in other tubes all throughout here, Clarity's Dawn is sending all they've got into this fight.

Or rather, they will. We're going in first. Start with a surprise, one that the Sevora won't see coming, and that ought to give us a real shot at getting out.

"Anyone think this has a chance?" Viera says as we ride.

"It has a better one than sitting down there," I reply. "And at least, this time, we get what we want."

"Right. Because instead of being kept out of the fighting, we're bait instead. Just what I was hoping for."

Sapphrite's plan had called for us to act as a draw, a distracting target for Sevora while the real work went on elsewhere. Clarity's Dawn would keep us safe, Sapphrite said, and then deliver us to the spaceport after.

Problem is, I'm not a fan anymore of 'after', of 'trust'. There isn't any guarantee that Clarity's Dawn won't use us as pawns after the mission. So instead, Malo and I made some recommendations. Swapped some places.

"This gives us the best chance of escape," Malo says. "We're in control of our own destiny now, rather than someone else."

"I believe I'm controlling your destiny right this moment, Malo," T'Oli notes cheerfully from the controls. "Could turn this thing right around, or stop it and let us all plummet to a messy end."

"But you wouldn't do that, T'Oli," I acknowledge the joke. "Because that would hurt your Beast."

"True enough," T'Oli replies. "Did I tell you how long it took me to clean her out?"

"Yes," all of us reply in unison.

"It was a monster job, is all I'm getting at."

I reach for my scalp again, catch Malo's eyes and pull my hand away. I haven't seen him make a single twitch towards his own black hair. Suppose that warrior discipline comes in handy sometimes.

"Did we decide who gets to fly our ship when we steal it? Assuming we get that far?" Viera asks after another few minutes of trundling.

"I've got the Cache. I'll use it."

"So you're going to fall into one of your trances right when we're running from a bunch of angry enemies?"

"Do you have a better plan?" Malo asks, leaning around me. "Are you equipped to fly one of these things?"

"I grew up with gadgets under the mountains," Viera replies. "I can figure it out."

"Then we'll call it when we get there," I say. "There's only so far a plan can go, anyway."

"You just don't want me to have any fun," Viera pouts. "Get stabbed by Malo, captured by Oratus, imprisoned by Sevora, the list goes on and on."

"But look at what you're wearing? Doesn't that count?"

Viera's sporting a new set of synthetic armor over her mask, though its mismatched colors give away the fact that it's a blend of other sets. After all, Vimelia doesn't exactly have human-sized gear, seeing as they didn't know we existed. What I'm really focused on are the pair of shiny miners, scrubbed clean and bolted onto latches around Viera's waist. There's a chance the Sevora might take them away, but if we're lucky, she'll keep them.

"Guess you're right," Viera glances down at herself. "I did get the best outfit." She looks over at us, does a theatrical head shake. "Kaishi, what are you even wearing? A robe?"

It's a simple, brown-green sheet. With the mask on underneath, I just need something to keep the Sevora from recognizing I'm coated in the mask's invisible shell. If there's one thing I'm not concerned about right now, it's fashion.

"And Malo? Did you fall into a fire?"

He's sporting the thickest set of all of us, mostly because Malo's got the frame to support some of the same gear given to heavier Flaum. Like Viera says, though, most of it's blasted-black, a relic of prior battles and hasty repairs.

Rackt told Malo not to bet on it holding up in a fight, but they didn't have anything better to offer, so Malo took it.

T'Oli drops us near the surface, though there's still plenty of muck for us to slog through before getting to one of the wide ladders up.

"At least I felt clean for a day," Viera says as the brown stuff once again clutters up our clothes and the stench overtakes any pleasant memories my nose ever had.

There's a reason for this, though—if we're going to be convincing as survivors who've scrounged in the Vimelia sewers, we can't look refreshed and clean. So we're properly filthy by the time Malo pushes open the surface hatch and we find ourselves once more in the chaotic wonder of Vimelia's streets. Admittedly, I'm a fan of seeing the beige-white sky after so much time underground. Just feeling a true breeze and knowing that I'm not trapped inside something sparks energy and a smile.

"Don't know how you manage to live this way," I say to Viera as I stretch out my arms.

"It's what we know," Viera replies. "And it's not all bad—hard to sneak up on somebody in a cave."

Viera's looking past us and we turn to see a pair of Whelk wielding what look like long, thin tools operating on a panel embedded in the side of the tall, shimmering green structure we've emerged next to.

Only the Whelk aren't working anymore—they're staring at us with slack faces. I give them a wave—we are, after all, supposed to be caught—and finally one of them reaches for a circular device in a pouch around its body. Pulls it out and begins yammering into it.

"Suppose we just wait now?" Viera says.

"That is the plan," Malo replies, though he edges closer to me. He's still got that staff with him and I'm glad for it.

The goal might be to get captured, but it's not to get killed.

We don't have to wait long, however, before the Sevora announce themselves through a whirring roar. Above us, a narrow shuttle makes its way between the buildings and, out of a pair of opening bay doors, a squad of twelve armored Flaum—bearing Nasiya's emblems—drop down.

At first I think they're all going to fall and crush themselves on the ground, but their boots flare up as the Flaum close and they wind up floating just above the surface.

I recognize the primary one—black with white tufts—as the one that greeted us when we first touched down on Vimelia. It's obvious the Flaum hasn't forgotten us either, as he doesn't take any chances.

"Keep your limbs raised and clear," the Flaum barks at us as his troops go through the whole surrounding song and dance.

We're relieved of our weapons in short order, then to my surprise, we're walked out of the alleyway and along the main streets. Shuttles and other craft buzz above and alongside us, stopping ever-so-briefly to get a look at the strange new species.

"Why aren't we flying?" I manage to ask the Flaum after we've taken a few steps.

"You're close enough to walk," the Flaum replies.

"Close enough to what?"

"Nasiya demands no more chances," the Flaum replies. "Even if you can't be directly controlled, you will be influenced. You're receiving your masters today," the Flaum says, and there's a hint of pride in his voice.

That's when I realize that T'Oli wasn't taking us to a random drop point—no, this close to the surface, T'Oli deposited us next to a Sevora Host Center. Probably not it's actual name, but that's what I'm choosing to call the massive, long and flat space the Flaum guide us to.

Unlike the other buildings, this one is painted sky-blue and, atop its flat surface, has long winding spires that tilt towards each other and bind together around the center of the building.

"Unity," the Flaum says as we approach the doors. "No matter what divisions exist among the Sevora people, these spaces are sacrosanct. All who enter here do so to enrich their lives, and those of their hosts. Be thankful that you are going to receive one of the greatest gifts the Sevora can give."

"I can't wait," Viera mutters.

The way Lan says the words triggers a soft alarm in Sax's mind—there's caution there, wariness. Suspicion.

"You're here to rescue us?" Bas says.

"To see if you're still on the good side," Gar replies. "Or if you're with Evva."

"What happened to her?" Sax heads off that conversation, twists it. No sense in revealing his allegiance this early, with this little information.

"Stole a shuttle, vanished with a prisoner." Lan nods back towards the very shuttle they came in on. "Like this one. Any guesses as to who the prisoner was?"

"Avan." Sax's answer isn't a guess.

Gar nods. "Never would've thought the commander would fall for a Sevora. But I guess losing your pair messes you up."

"If I ever lost you," Lan says to Gar. "I'd . . . probably be more relaxed."

"You'd be bored, and you know it."

"She doesn't love Avan," Sax hisses. "Evva would never."

"Save it for the Amigga," Lan says. "If you know anything about her, where she might be—"

"They haven't found her yet?"

"Not yet," Gar says. "But they will. She's the top priority now. They're taking resources away from the Sevora to find her."

Why? Sax wants to ask this too, but he's getting the feeling that Lan and Gar are doing more than just picking two lost Oratus up from a rogue station. Neither one seems relaxed, both keep their midclaws on their miners, as if expecting an ambush at any moment.

"What's going to happen if we get on that shuttle?" Sax asks.

"If?" Lan replies.

"You heard me."

"You'll be debriefed. Asked about Evva. Prove that you're not on her side, and I'm sure they'll let you back in."

"Who's they?" Bas hisses.

Now Lan and Gar tense for a moment. Clear. The kind of movement Sax would expect to see from someone who hates their situation but who's trying to pass it off as bearable. The kind of movement he's seen from people who need rescuing.

"The Chorus sent Amigga to every cruiser," Lan says. "To preserve the loyalty of the fleet."

"They've interrogated everyone, even the Flaum and Whelk." Gar adds. "It's stupid, but once you're clear, it's over."

Sax wonders what'll happen when the Amigga find out he's burned one of their number to an ashen crisp. He thought the Amigga on *Cobalt* had lost its mind, but there's no guarantee any others would see it that way. Which means he and Bas could be going into a trap. But if they try to stay on the station, then . . . they couldn't survive here either. Sax sees only one option: try to find Evva. Right back where they started.

"What if we say no?" Sax asks.

"No to what?"

"Getting on that shuttle with you. Going back to the Vincere."

That stiffens their spines. Tenses their arms. Sax lets his teeth show just a bit. Feels Bas' tail touch his, wrap its end around the tip of his own. She's with him, whatever comes.

"That would be a dangerous choice," Lan says finally. "They would order us to bring you in. By force."

"Do you think you could?" Sax counters.

"Sax, I've always wanted a good brawl with you," Gar rasps. "But not here, not like this."

"Then let us walk away," Sax replies. "Because I'm not getting on that shuttle. The Vincere isn't what it was, and I'm not liking the new look."

In a flash, Lan and Gar have their miners raised, pointed at Sax.

"Bas, don't be like him," Lan hisses. "You don't have to pay for his choices."

Bas laughs. "The thing about pairs, Lan, is that I do."

It takes a long moment to pull the trigger on a friend, on someone that you've ridden with into the bleakest of fights, the deadliest of environments. Whose life you've saved and whose saved your life more times than either of you remember.

Sax and Bas use that moment—they both slide to the side, turning and flicking their tails at the miners Lan and Gar are holding. Batter the weapons away from the claws and send them clattering to the floor.

Gar springs at Sax, claws outstretched, mouth opening in a wide, hissing roar. Sax, body angled aside from Gar, catches and throws the oncoming Oratus pass him. Feels a cut across his midsection as Gar's talons go by.

Gar, though, smashes into the ground, rolls against the wide door leading back into the station and, digging grooves into the metal floor, turns himself around and launches back at Sax. The two Oratus are nearly the same size, and Sax can see the blind bloodlust has taken Gar's senses.

It's going to be a raw brawl.

So Sax jumps forward, meets Gar in mid-air and the two crash to the ground, rolling and snapping and clawing at each other. It's a rush of instinct—a flash of claw here, glistening teeth biting there—and at the end of it, when Gar winds up on the bottom and kicks Sax off, both are bleeding. Both are grinning.

Ready for the next round.

"Never took you for a traitor," Gar hisses as the two circle each other.

"Always took you for a bloodthirsty maniac," Sax replies.

He wants to see how Bas is doing, help her, but looking away from Gar for even a second could prove fatal. All Sax has to go on are hissing sounds behind him, the crash and rumble as heavy bodies crash into things.

"You were right," Gar laughs, and then the Oratus launches—

No. A feint.

Sax bites, though. Jerks forward to meet a leap that isn't coming as Gar reaches behind his back and pulls another miner from his mask. Aims, fires. Sax has a split second to move and doesn't clear the shot, which powers into his left leg.

It goes numb. Not the burn of a killing laser, but the blue ice of a stunning shot.

"You want us alive?"

"The Commander thinks you might know where Evva's heading, what she's after." Gar raises the miner again as Sax keeps limping, trying to get towards a long rack of batteries. "Personally, Sax, I'd rather not kill you."

"I'm not getting on that shuttle, Gar," Sax hisses.

He gets close to the batteries—there in case a ship's dead and needs a burst of energy—when Gar fires again. Hits Sax's back, and now almost everything's lost feeling. Sax falls forward, his head jutting against the rack.

"Don't think you have a choice," Gar says, though the Oratus doesn't shift closer.

A smart move. Keep your distance when you've only got a small miner and a big target. Stunning's an imprecise science. Better to overdo it.

Gar raises the miner again. Aims for Sax's head.

"Sleep well," the Oratus hisses.

And Sax, with the flickering connection in his left foreclaw, throws a battery at Gar as the Oratus pulls the trigger.

A bright blue-white burst engulfs the universe for a quick moment and Sax's eyes dazzle in the light. His mind goes fuzzy, and the only thing he does, for longer than he'd like, is lay there and try to reconnect with the rest of himself. That much super-charged electricity could have killed him, probably would have if Sax wasn't an Oratus. If he didn't have two hearts and layer after layer of thick muscle, protective scales, and a half-mask catching what it can of the blast.

Gar, though, fares worse. The battery, freed from its enclosure and nearly to the Oratus by the time the trigger depresses, catches Gar with the full force of its fury. The physical push of the blast has knocked the Oratus on his back, but what's more evident is that Gar has no control of himself at all. His body is a wriggling mess as synapses run wild. The other weapons on him short circuit too— exploding or melting with a variety of pops and sparks, burning through the mask or melting into boiling puddles on the floor around him.

Not that Gar's stuck there for long—Sax, whose head is lying on the floor staring at his distressed former friend, sees Lan dash into view. Sees her scoop Gar up and lope away from the broken remnants of his weaponry. She pauses for a moment, glances towards what Sax believes is Bas, though he can't turn his head to look.

"You're broken now," Lan says. "You're on the wrong side."

"Did Evva ever do you wrong?" Bas hisses back. "Did she ever send us on a bad mission, or leave us to die? Why would she do this now, unless she had a reason?"

"Our job, the whole reason we live, is to support the Chorus. Do as they say, fight as they command." Lan keeps backing towards the shuttle, Gar in her arms. "Turn your back on them, and you've denied your reason for being."

"Your reason, maybe," Bas says. "But not ours. Go back to your ship, Lan. Tell them what's happened. We'll be here when you return."

"We won't come back alone. You'll be outnumbered. Captured and hauled before the Amigga as traitors. As dishonorable a death as you can imagine."

"Fighting for what we believe? You have a strange notion of honor." Bas appears in front of Sax, kneeling over him. Sniffs him quick, then reaches beneath Sax with her claws and lifts him up.

Lan and Gar get on the platform, which rises up into the belly of the shuttle. Bas doesn't stay to watch, lugging Sax from the docking bay, towards the lifts out of the spoke.

"We're going back to Plake," Bas hisses as they move. "Her ship is our best shot at getting out of here now."

Sax tries to agree, but his mouth doesn't work. So instead he lies in his pair's arms, and hopes the next fight won't come too soon.

"Why should I help you again?" Plake says, this time on the *Mobius*.

Coorvin led Sax and Bas up onto the ship, where Agra-Red waited with his new heavy miner in hand. Apparently Plake didn't want to be seen talking with the two most-wanted Oratus on *Scrapper Station*.

"Because of what we'll bring you," Bas says.

Sax is slowly recovering—he's able to control his own breathing now, and he can use his muscles to keep himself upright, if not walk with any stability. Still, he tries to look strong, even as a bit of drool escapes his numb jaw and plops down to the floor.

Plake eyes it, then looks up at Bas, "What's that, besides a ton of angry soldiers?"

"You said you hate the Oratus. The Amigga. That you want to see them beaten."

"Lots of people wish for the impossible, doesn't mean I'm trying to make it happen."

Bas breaks into a quick story about Avan, the Sevora traitor that promised galaxy-changing secrets. About how Evva's escaped with him, about how if Plake helps Sax and Bas reunite with their commander, they might be able to . . . do something.

"You don't even know these secrets?" Plake laughs. "Avan might be playing all of you. Another Sevora trick to get deep into our society."

"The Sevora was sincere," but even Bas can't put much force in this one.

"Look, Oratus. I don't like you. I'm not going to risk my crew and my own life on your crazy idea, which may be nothing!" Plake nods at Agra-Red. "Get them out of here. With any luck, the military will take care of them and leave us alone."

"Mistake," Sax manages to rasp. Weak, but it's there.

"Oh, he can talk now?" Plake shakes her head. "Too late. Leave."

Agra-Red doesn't give Sax another chance to argue. Forces the both of them out of the ship, keeping its miner trained on them the entire way. Then, once the two Oratus are on the floor, the ramp raises up and seals them out.

"That didn't go as I hoped," Bas says as she pulls Sax out of the bay. "There's only one other place we can try."

The Sisters let them in, let them up the lift back to their beautiful garden. Now, though, the Oratus frigate wipes through the viewing window every so often, spoiling any sense of peace. Rather than taking the Oratus to their building, the Sisters, with Eneks and a couple of armed Flaum that Sax recognizes from the casino, greet the Oratus immediately as they come off the lift.

"Your circumstances aren't good," L'Reneo says.

"Not good at all," N'Ollene adds.

"That's why we're here," Bas says. "For help."

And by the way the Sisters eyestalks swivel, by the rapid clatter of their Ooblot forms, Sax knows they're in trouble.

Getting your feeling back is like waking from a dream—gradually, reality filters in. Your feet get their traction, your talons passing along the usual edge as they dig small cuts into the floor. Your vents open wider and wider, and you can actually feel the air rejuvenate your muscles. Your tail twitches when you want it to, and your four claws start to open and close on command instead of by nervous whims.

Sax gets all this back in time to hear the Sisters laugh in Bas' face, in time to see the Flaum guards pull their miners up while the lift doors behind them shut.

"The Vincere's offered good terms for you," L'Renee says. "We hold you here, they come get you, and *Scrapper Station* gets forgotten about for a long, long time. Know what it's worth not having to deal with Vincere inspections?"

"They wouldn't," N'Ollene says. "They're not one of us. Not normal people."

Sax squeezes Bas' shoulder slightly, lets her know that he's back, most of the way. She keeps holding him, though, because if there's one thing to keep hidden, it's an Oratus surprise.

"So if you'd follow our friends to the airlock, there, we'll be keeping you safe and sound till they come pick you up," L'Renee says.

"A nice ride home," N'Ollene adds.

The Flaum gesture with their miners and Bas pulls them both along. Across the garden towards the airlock. Every step brings another iota of feeling back, every step makes Sax a deadlier weapon.

The Sisters order the two Oratus into the airlock, with Eneks again stepping up to open the door. It shunts ajar, leaving a gleaming cream tube waiting. Stepping into that tube means death, a slow and awful one once the Amigga find neither Sax nor Bas knows where Evva is. And death by torture, death in captivity is not one Sax will stand.

He pushes off of Bas, sending her flying to the side and uses the momentum to pivot and leap at the first Flaum. The furry guard fires, but the shot's hopelessly wide of the crouched, scrambling Oratus.

The Flaum doesn't get a second one.

Sax turns from his downed target to see Bas splitting apart the other guard's miner, a scorch mark on her right shoulder. The Sisters, meanwhile, are running away with Eneks, rolling across the grass towards their building.

It's a futile effort.

"You'll stop, or you'll die," Sax hisses as he catches up to them, the Flaum's miner in his right midclaw. The weapon's not made for Oratus hands, but at this range, accuracy doesn't matter so much. He'll just spray lasers until they submit, or burn.

They choose the former, huddling up together and staring at their new captor. Eneks fades from his blue color to a sickly purple, and picks at his feathers while his bulbous eyes blink. Sax isn't used to having hostages. The normal Oratus position is that an enemy is better off dead, preferably eaten. Not captive.

The Sisters, apparently, can see his hesitance.

"What will you do now?" L'Renee asks. "Keep us here until your Vincere comes anyway and takes you away?"

"Or will you shoot us and wind up the same?" N'Ollene adds.

"We'll do neither," Bas replies, stepping up beside Sax.

She's not wielding a miner, but there's also no sign of the Flaum she tangled with. It's as dead as Sax's, or she's chased it off. Either way, the odds of the Sisters and their Vyphen pal making it away alive are growing dimmer.

"This station must have some defenses, yes?" Bas asks.

"Nothing major." Eneks hazards a reply. "It's not meant for fighting."

"But to ward off pirates? Certainly a place like this is a raid target."

Again the Sisters squirm, patter towards each other.

"Speak so we all can hear," Sax says.

"We have weapons," L'Renee says. "But they're not for you to use."

"Never anyone but us," N'Ollene adds.

"You'll use them, then, to shoot the next shuttle they send," Bas says. "We'll get them to send it, and then you'll destroy it. And everything that comes after."

The Sisters laugh. Eneks even looks confused.

"You think they'll leave? The Vincere will never go away if we fire on them. They'll simply attack in greater and greater numbers until there's nothing left of this station."

Bas shrugs her claws. "That's your future. This is your now. Either you take us to the weapons and fire them, or you die here. If you want, you can blame the attack on us."

There's not much debate after that. The Sisters roll off across the garden, with Eneks and the Oratus following. Until they reach the building, which is far too small for any Oratus to enter. The Sisters, though, scramble inside before Sax can react.

Bas grabs Eneks before the Vyphen can try to run, leaving Sax to make the obvious threat. Either the Ooblots do as they've agreed, or their beloved servant becomes a messy stain in the middle of their garden.

"We're not running," L'Renee's voice comes from inside the building. "The only way to arm the station is in here."

"Where nobody else can get it," N'Ollene adds.

"Hold him?" Sax asks Bas.

"He's not going anywhere. Right, Eneks?"

The Vyphen shakes his head, feathers ruffling wildly. Sax takes the cue to jump on top of the building, where he tracks the Ooblots through the translucent roof, watches them shift through one room after another until they get to the back, to a small room where, after Sax digs his claws into the ceiling and pulls it off, he can see an array of terminals.

"What did you just do?" L'Renee protests.

"He's ruined our home!" N'Ollene says.

"Making sure you do as you're supposed to," Sax replies. "Tell them you've caught us. Have them send the shuttle towards the airlock."

The Sisters do as asked. It's Lan's voice on the receiving line, and she says a pickup will be on its way shortly. If both Lan and Gar are on that shuttle . . . getting ambushed and blown up in space isn't a good Oratus death either.

Sax flicks back towards Bas, whose still holding Eneks and looking bored with it. He has to protect her, just as she protects him. Sax tells the Sisters to go ahead, to arm the weapons.

He's going to start a war to save himself.

The inside is long, wide, and unbroken. And I recognize it. These are the same pools Ignos had me making back in Damantum—frothing purple liquid with textured lips to allow for easy in-and-out access. Only where we were building two or three, here there are easily a twenty, if not more.

The space is crowded too—all sorts of species are being herded around by Sevora-hosted Flaum and Whelk. Everyone's being pushed into various lines, though our Flaum guards keep us away from the rest of the throng and take us to the far end.

"No common Sevora for you," the Flaum leader continues. "You'll be receiving the best of hosts, experienced and capable. You should be honored."

"It's never an honor to lose your freedom," Malo replies.

"Then think of it as sacrifice, if you prefer," the Flaum replies. "What you're doing here is only going to help your people. By submitting to the Sevora, you will save them, either from yourselves or from the rest of a hungry, brutal galaxy."

"Is that the pitch you make to everyone?" Viera asks.

"Because it's not very good," I add. "You should try talking up the miracles you'll be giving us. How we'll never starve, how we won't need to worry about making our own choices, how we'll never have to want for anything ever again."

The Flaum stares at me for a moment, trying to decide if I'm joking or being serious.

"Or can the Sevora not grant all of our wishes?" I finish.

"We will change your wishes, and then grant them," the Flaum replies.

That's clearly enough talking for him, as he turns and heads along the outer edge of the pools, and his guards push us along after him.

As we go, I look to the right and see a lanky Teven slowly walk towards a pool, its tiny limbs sticking out from the long reed serving as its central body. It hesitates about halfway across the pearly flagstones and a Flaum comes up behind it, reaches out with a clawed hand and pushes the Teven forward.

The Teven whirls at the touch and for a second I think it's going to mount some kind of resistance, but then the Flaum raises his miner and the Teven decides not to risk its life in the face of the laser cannon. It turns, wades into the pool and disappears beneath the purple waters.

"How many do you take every day?" I ask the Flaum, because I'm realizing if I don't talk, then I might panic.

"Thousands across Vimelia are exchanged daily," the Flaum replies, once again falling into his boastful tone. "Whether we're recycling old hosts, integrating new ones, or trading one Sevora to another to better match needs, the Sevora are always in motion."

I first met Ignos in a crashed pod outside my tribe, deep in the jungle. When I approached its ship, thinking it was a rock, it opened and, inside, was an inky liquid much like what I see in these pools. I went in, and gained what I thought was a god, what was in fact a creature determined to spread its parasitic race across my world. Here, though, the event seems so commonplace. As if giving up everything to another species is as normal as cooking breakfast or running through the trees.

It twists my stomach into tight knots, and I take a hard swallow to get my breath back. Feel Malo's hand touch my arm lightly and breathe easier for it. I'm not alone this time.

There's no line for our pool, and as we approach, the Flaum asks us who ought to go first.

Malo volunteers immediately, but I shut him down.

"Let me," I say. "I've done this before, and I know what to expect. If something's wrong, I'll be able to deal with it."

"Nothing will go wrong," the Flaum says, nodding across the hall. "This is the most common thing we do. It's the very core of who the Sevora are. Now, get in and submit."

There's not much in the way of ceremony for entering a Sevora pool. The Flaum don't care if I keep on my clothes—I don't know if they realize I'm wearing a mask—and they don't blow horns, flash lights, or do anything other than watch me with their hands close to their miners.

Malo and Viera watch me too, of course, though their faces are etched with concern. Even though this is part of the plan, we all know it's not going to be pleasant.

The flagstones are cool to the touch, and everything glows somewhat in the clear light filtering in from the roof, which is a translucent cover that provides a frankly amazing view of all those intertwining spires. Not for the first time I'm surprised at how much beauty these terrible things can create.

I get up to the edge and look into the purple. It's too dark to see below the surface, the water quickly getting to the level of a deep twilight. There's clearly current too—either that or the Sevora themselves make the ripples caressing the surface.

"Get in," the Flaum barks from behind me. "Your master needs its host."

Apparently that's the cue. I take the order and step forward, expecting there to be a step but there isn't one. It's just a cliff. I overbalance, send out a yelp, and splash into the pool.

That's me, always dignified.

I try to swim, but the liquid is heavy, pulling me down. As though

I'm trying to shove against the same thick muck that coated the sewers. Every stroke tightens my muscles and leaves me sinking, to the point where I wonder if I'll just drown in here.

The thought dies a swift death as I feel a tickling touch around my head. I try to lift a hand to brush it away, but the ink is too thick down here, too heavy. I can't even get my arm up that high. Not that it matters anyway—Sapphrite's big design gets to work before the probing Sevora can realize my mask is blocking it.

The sign comes when the ink around me starts to shift color, to bloom into a sickly orange as the coating on my hair reacts with the nourishing chemicals in the ink and grows. Spreads its viral haze through the pool.

At once the tickling touch vanishes—if Sapphrite's creation works, that same virus should be devouring the Sevora now, gobbling up the thin-skinned parasite and spreading from this pool to the others.

Of course, the mask protects me from the virus too. Its protection is what made Malo, Viera, and I such perfect vessels for the delivery. As it is, though, I'm stuck at the bottom of a massively growing collection of voracious cells, and I can't lift myself out.

There's a shift next to me and I see the Flaum guard's gray-metal stick slash through the thick orange like a black line. I'm able to get my hands around it, the mask protecting me from the rough edges, and I feel myself start to rise.

Like a parting film, the orange gives way as I reach the surface to total chaos. Shouts pour in through the mask, coupled with far-off bangs.

Clarity's Dawn is beginning their part of the deal.

Malo grabs my arm and pulls me the rest of the way out, and I get my first look at what's happening to the rest of the pools.

Sapphrite said the bacteria would spread fast, hopefully fast enough to outrun any seals the Sevora could enact. Right now, more than half of the pools are turning orange as the stuff eats its way through the pipes that apparently connect them all.

Sevora-controlled guards are running around in a panic, heading for panels or just fleeing entirely as captive species realize they have a sudden chance to be free.

"They will seize their opportunity," Sapphrite said back down below. "They will fight back once they've seen what's coming for them."

In this case, anyway, the Amigga is right. After seeing what waits in those pools, and with the guards distracted, Teven, Whelk, Flaum and others rush either towards exits or towards their captors, angling to pull miners from their hands.

But not all of them. Some simply stand still, looking around, vacant-eyed and lost.

"We've got to go," Viera says, and I turn away from the scene to see my friend with both of her miners drawn, picked up from a pile of taken tools and weapons meant to be directly returned once a Sevora has taken control of their new host.

There's only one exit from the building that I can see, and it's crowded with bodies and the flashes of miners, though whether the attacks are coming from Sevora or not, I can't tell.

"Not that way." I point back behind the tubes, towards a set of maintenance doors, where some of the Sevora guards had disappeared. "They won't be expecting us to head through the back."

At first, at least, nobody stops us. With Viera leading and Malo watching behind, the three of us break around the long pool towards those doors. They're smaller than human entries, smaller too than the ones on *Cobalt*, which must have been sized with Oratus in mind. These are simple squares about two meters high, plenty tall for a Flaum but Malo has to duck under as we head through them.

That the doors open straight away surprises me, until I remember that the Sevora operate by absolute authority. Why bother with security when everyone on the planet ought to be under your iron-fisted control?

Beyond the door I expect to find hallways, but instead it's another open area, and what I see is horrifying: rows and rows of stunned species clumped together. Bodies of Flaum, Whelk and others piled on one another, though they're all seemingly still alive. Still breathing, though they barely move.

"You're a host for so long, you don't know how to be free," Viera says, and even her light voice carries lead at the sight.

"This, this is what happens?" I say the words knowing neither of them can answer, knowing that I'm seeing it all spread before me.

There are shallow pools on this side too—much smaller, and many of the bodies are clustered outside of them. Where the Sevora must evacuate their hosts before heading to the other side for new ones. No secret why they'd want to keep these pools hidden , either—any captive looking at these bodies would get a very different idea of what it means to be a Sevora host.

And that's when I realize why some of the Sevora guards went this way—there are so many listless souls here that if someone roused them to fight, they could overwhelm this whole building and more.

"Hundreds and hundreds of them," Malo whispers.

"Come on," I finally muster. "We can't just watch or the Sevora will realize we're not taken. Let's go."

The shot fires—a blast of bright white hot energy streaking out towards the approaching Oratus shuttle. Just when it's about to hit, the white bolt diffuses into a series of thin crackles and scatters around the ship without any apparent damage.

"Dispersion shields," Bas hisses. "They suspected."

"How could they not? Two Ooblots catching two Oratus?" Eneks says. "Especially ones like yourselves?"

Sax watches the shuttle continue its approach, heading in towards the garden's airlock. If the ship had its shields running—something that drained plenty of energy, and not worth doing if you didn't suspect an attack—then it followed that whatever waited inside that shuttle would be strong enough to take Sax and Bas by force.

"Fire again," Sax orders, and the Ooblots carry out the order.

Another white bolt lances out, another white bolt dissipates into nothing.

"You only have one cannon on this station?" Sax asks.

"Only one that we're willing to use," Eneks replies. "Try to kill us if you want, but if we make enemies of the Vincere, then we are most definitely dead."

"We need to run, Sax," Bas says. "Back to Plake, maybe? Force her to take us away?"

Sax is shaking his head before Bas is done talking. He's had enough of negotiations. Enough deals and dancing around. There's only one way he wants to get out of this—Sax wants to fight, to win, to get back who he is.

"Eneks, where is the nearest communications array?" Sax hisses and the Vyphen points towards another room in the Ooblot's short building.

"What are you doing?" L'Renee asks.

"It can't be good!" N'Ollene adds.

Sax clomps into the Ooblot's space. The terminals are set low, but Sax can still tap the screens, still open a channel to the oncoming shuttle.

"This is Sax, your target," Sax rasps into the speakers inset in the terminal's base.

"You're wanted for suspected rebellion against the Chorus," the voice that comes back is watery, a Whelk. "You're ordered to stand down and await our arrival. Any further attempts at attack from the station will be returned with lethal force."

"Torching an entire station for two Oratus seems brutal, even by our standards," Sax says.

"We follow our orders, unlike you."

"I follow my conscience." Sax cuts the communication. Flips the channel to broadcast through the station. "*Scrapper Station*, the Vincere is declaring that anyone on this station who does not submit for an interrogation, who does not give themselves up and face whatever crimes they may be guilty of, will be shot dead."

He takes a breath. Looks back at Bas, who gives him the nod.

A lie that might cause many to die.

A lie that might let the Oratus live.

"We've chosen to fight back. Any who stand with us, who want to survive, find your weapons, form up, and find your courage. *Scrapper Station* will not bow to oppression!"

Inciting innocents to rebel isn't something Sax has ever done before, and being up in the garden, away from those same people, makes it hard to discern what effect he's had, if any. The key, though, is that he added an open channel to that last broadcast, sent it flying out into space.

To the Vincere frigate, to the shuttle.

If there's guilt to be had in potentially setting up a fight between people who could have avoided it, Sax kills it with the sure knowledge that anyone on *Scrapper Station* is likely avoiding lawful work anyway. Everyone here has something to hide, someone to scam, and a willingness to do whatever it takes to survive.

What he's betting on is that they'll do enough to buy Sax and Bas some time to find a way off of this station.

"At least we'll keep our promise to the Teven," Bas says as Sax returns to them.

"Yes, I'm sure they'll be thrilled when the entire station is burning because of your actions." Eneks sighs.

"You've killed us all!" L'Renee shouts from her terminal.

"Only if you let them," Sax says. "It's either fight or die now, Ooblot."

"Then we fight!" N'Ollene announces. "Fire, Sister, and fire again!"

This time, it's five white bursts lancing forth from the station, and now the shuttle tries to move. It jockeys up and down, so that only three of the shots manage to splash across its shields, with the last punching through and glancing off the shuttle's armor.

"Aim for the frigate," Sax says. "Keep it away from the station. We'll handle the shuttle."

"I don't like this," L'Renee replies.

"But we'll try," N'Ollenne adds.

Sax and Bas lope over to the airlock as the shuttle screams in for a hard docking. Two Oratus against who knows how many. Sax still has the miner he took from the Flaum guard, but that's hardly enough artillery. They check around the airlock, looking for vulnerabilities, for places to set up in cover, but the bushes won't block any lasers, and the airlock is wide enough to let the troops stream through.

"Our only chance is breaking the seal," Bas says as they study the airlock, looking for hope.

"We don't have the weapons to do that," Sax replies.

"But we do," Agra-Red's voice comes from behind them. The fiery whelk's assault miner, built into its body, has a full set of batteries lacing from the weapon and around Agra-Red. Black, the burly female Flaum, stands next to him, along with Plake, each holding oodles of their own weaponry.

And they're all aiming at the two Oratus.

"What do you think, Plake?" Agra-Red says. "We blast them, the Vincere lets us all go?"

The Vyphen captain brushes her purple-red mouth with an iridescent feathered arm, then shakes her head. "Feel like that option's already gone. These two have torched all of us. That's what happens when you fire on a Vincere ship. They'll just raze the station rather than take stock of who's innocent and who's not."

Sax is trying to find a vulnerability, but unlike the useless Flaum guards from earlier, Plake, Black, and Agra-Red are keeping their distance. They'd have more than enough time to react, aim, and fire before Sax could leap to them.

"That's the point," Bas hisses. "We told you. There's something bigger going on here, something that ends if Evva gets captured."

"Big enough to damn everyone on this station?" Plake says.

"Yes."

The Vyphen puts on a show of considering, but Sax bets she's already made up her mind. He's thinking if Plake really wanted them dead, she'd have shot them in the back. Not even given him or Bas a chance to respond.

"Here's what I'm looking at," Plake starts. "The rest of my life spent running nutrient goop and stopping in dives like this one, or a short burst spent trying to hurt the bastards who've turned the Vyphen into cretins like this one."

She nods at Eneks, who manages to look both offended and embarrassed at the same time.

"The Oratus torched my homeworld," Agra-Red says. "I've got no love for them. No love for you two, either, but it sounds like you might give me a shot at doing some real damage." It twists, aiming the assault miner behind Sax. "Besides, I need more excuses to play with this thing."

Both of them look at Black, who's wielding a snub-nosed gouter, hooked to a big tank on her back. She looks at the Oratus and shrugs.

"Coorvin says you're on the good side, and I trust him."

There's a loud thunk from behind them, followed by the whirring and clacking sounds of locks sliding into place. The shuttle's docking.

"Now get out of the way, you morons, or I'll fry you too," Agra-Red waves the tip of its miner, and both Sax and Bas break to either side of the airlock door.

Eneks dashes to the airlock's control panel, glances back at Plake, who shakes her head.

"Not until they're inside," Plake says. "We've only got one shot at this."

Sax watches through the glass into the white cream of the airlock. Instead of a real window opening to space, there's now a tunnel lit by small globe lights. A tunnel that leads back to the shuttle, to the force coming to take them all.

Though, going by Agra-Red's manic grin, Sax thinks the Vincere's going to have a harder time than expected.

The first Flaum troops pour into the airlock, and they're ready for almost anything. They've got miners, they've got armor, and they're moving like a trained squad. What they're not expecting, though, is a mad red Whelk with a giant cannon waiting for them.

At Plake's nod, Eneks opens the panel and, as the airlock door shunts aside, Agra-Red opens up. A cascade of red bolts pours forth, punctuated by a rising whine as the weapon's pumps keep working to churn gas through the miner's ionizing batteries. Agra-Red keeps the steady spray moving back and forth, and, beyond the panicked screams of trapped Flaum, there's a new sound: vacuum alarms. Agra-Red's pierced the shell leading back to the shuttle, exposing everything to open space.

At the first hint of the pull, the airlock slams shut of its own accord and Sax doesn't even move a centimeter. The Flaum, and anyone caught in the tunnel to the shuttle, isn't so lucky. They're blasted out into space, and Sax can see their flash-frozen figures spiraling away into the black.

"Seal it," Plake says.

Black steps forward with her gouter and starts a spray of heavy green liquid. It splashes around the airlock, letting loose plenty of steam as the plasma burrows into the metal. The cooling comes rapidly, with the green settling into a deep gray and hardening around the door, eventually encasing the entire entrance.

"They can break that," Sax says.

"But they won't," Plake counters. "Not when they have plenty of docking bays to use."

There's a crackle, then L'Renee's voice echoes over the station's broadcast system, "They're launching additional shuttles and fighters. *Scrapper Station*, get ready for imminent assault!"

"Show them what a bunch of scuzzy lowlifes and vagabonds can do!" N'Ollene adds.

They don't waste time hanging around the airlock. All five of them—Eneks retreats back to the Sisters—head to the lift, hustle in, and take it down to the Nexus.

"Never expected you to come to our defense," Sax says as the lift chugs lower.

"Never wanted to," Plake replies. "You forced our hand."

"We meant to."

"That's not what you're supposed to say."

"Thank you," Bas hisses. "Now, we have to leave."

Agra-Red laughs. "Leave? After you've got them all riled up?"

"Even if we manage to hold back this assault," Bas says. "They'll be calling for reinforcements. The station will be destroyed, unless we get away. Unless we claim responsibility."

"Compassion? From an Oratus? I didn't think you had any," Plake says, then sighs. "And I suppose you're planning on us to take you?"

"Yes."

Sax isn't much for subtlety.

We make it all of ten steps. We're next to one of the feeder pools, a quartet of Whelk standing, looking at us with nothing going on in their eyes, when there's a yell from further down the room.

"The humans came this way!" The Flaum's voice is hard, angry and bright. "Leave these, get them!"

It looks like the Flaum's group is busy shooting freed, confused species and tossing them into piles. Summary executions for potential problems. Seeing it makes me feel sick, but I suppress the revulsion when I see the ten Flaum turn our way.

"And now we run," Viera says.

Part of me wants to stay and fight, because it's clear the sort of end coming to all of these innocents. Clear the Sevora are choosing harsh security, that they're treating these species as products rather than people. But we're outnumbered and outgunned, and if there's going to be this much death, then the sacrifice ought to be for something.

Viera fires a few shots from her miners, though I don't see if any hit. I'm looking around, trying to find an exit, and locate one along the back wall; a series of arched doors similar to the ones in Nasiya's tower, the ones leading to those tubes and the white platforms.

"That way! Through the arches!" I shout as I break into a run.

In the jungle, I used trees for cover, whether to hide or to dodge thrown rocks and fired arrows. Here I do the same, only instead of trees, I use the ambling forms of stupefied Flaum, of clustered Tevens just beginning to flex their arms and legs outside their carapaces. The Sevora Flaum fire away, and they don't care where their miners burn. Species drop around us as we run, many without a sound. Maybe they're so divorced from their own feelings that they don't even recognize pain.

Bolts that don't hit a bystander zing into the walls and floor around us, leaving scorch marks or bubbling tile.

A shot lands right in front of me, exploding a chunk of the floor, and the hot dust blasts my face, the mask blunting the temperature. I stumble, though the mask filters away the dust, then feel Malo's arm on my back, pushing me forward.

"If we stop, Kaishi, we die," he says, and I want to tell him I know but can't find the breath.

The air is sick with burning flesh, with the electric zap of molten metal and discharged batteries and my mask doesn't clean out the smell. My ears ring with shouts, the whine of energy being spent, and the constant rumble of explosions outside the building.

But we make the arches. Me first, with Malo just behind, and Viera continuing her stream of wild shots. I notice the armor on her has a few burn holes, but Viera's still moving and we don't have time for first aid anyway.

All the arches funnel into a back, smaller section that in turn feeds into those same platform tubes.

"The middle one!" I point as we run towards the only platform already there and waiting.

The rest of the station is empty—apparently nobody wants to visit the birthing pools when everything goes wrong. Lasers continue to splash into the walls behind us, but the pursuit seems half-hearted. By the time we reach the platform, there's nobody even in sight.

"Anyone know how to use this thing?" Viera asks as we stream through the doors.

"No idea," I say, turning to the control panel anyway. "But I'm guessing anywhere is better than here."

There's no buttons, only a screen with a maze of icons. It reminds me of the console on *Cobalt*, and I wish Ignos were here to tell me what they all meant. Lacking the Sevora, and lacking the time to dip into the Cache, I tap one that looks like a flying ship.

The doors slam shut. I step back onto the platform and sit in the chair that forms to match my size.

"We're alive," I manage to say to my friends, and then the platform rockets away.

Our ride launches us up and away from the birthing pool building, and what I see sears into my mind: across Vimelia's vast cityscape, towers of smoke rise from all over, like black, billowing trees from a silvery desert.

Unlike our first ride with the Flaum, this platform expands a transparent film around us as we get up to speed, and I find my breath isn't stolen away by the rapid air. Apparently the Sevora build their transport by grades—ones going to and from the birthing pools get a better class of ride.

"Sapphrite wasn't kidding," Viera says as we zip through the air. "Clarity's Dawn is going all out on this one."

"Did you see how it looked down there?" I reply. "They were starving, and it seemed like only luck was keeping them alive. Rather than wait for the Sevora to end them, better fight on their terms."

"Better to die for something than because of someone," Malo adds.

The tube swoops us out and around the large sculpture near the birthing pool building, and we get a good look at what's happening outside the main entrance, where most of the prisoners are scrambling.

It's just as bad as the way we went—a firing range of Sevora guards lays waste to unarmed, panicked prisoners trying to pile their way out of the building. A one-sided lightshow.

"That's so horrible," I can't keep from saying.

"Ignos wanted you to join that? No thanks." Viera glances at her miners. "You should have let me stomp the slug when Rackt took it out of your head."

"Maybe so."

The platform, mercifully, keeps moving and soon the slaughter disappears out of sight behind taller buildings. It's still hard to see where we're heading, so I tell the other two that I'm going to slip into the Cache.

Even with all the excitement, triggering the Cache and its emerald flash pulls me away from our zipping ride and into the infinite, cool nexus of data. Immediately a giant map of Vimelia fills the space around me, and our current location shows as a blinking dot in a translucent blue city.

The Cache traces out our current path, and it goes right from where we are towards a large oval that, with a mental question, the Cache identifies as the spaceport.

With our side of Sapphrite's mission done—all we had to do was poison the birthing pools—our only goal now is to get to the spaceport, find the shuttle that Rackt is supposed to have waiting for us, and get out of here.

I shake away the Cache and announce to Viera and Malo that we're going where we're supposed to. Settle back in and watch out the front.

Filling the air now are more and more of the Sevora shuttles that dropped the initial group of Flaum that met us when we escaped the sewers. Nasiya's emblem blazes on some, Jel's on others. Both factions, it seems, are coming together to stop Clarity's Dawn.

And I realize I don't really care anymore. Not about the Sevora struggle, not about Sapphrite's wish to live forever with the other

Amigga, or whether these creatures devour each other in their murderous politics. No, all I want is to go home.

Which is why I almost scream when the platform slows, then veers from its straight path to go down, right towards a tall, egg-shaped building beneath us. We shuttle through an opening in the top, big enough to only fit our single platform. The floors we pass by are dark, skeletal, as if this building is still under construction.

Eventually, the platform settles at the base, where, indeed, are piles and piles of materials.

There's also a set of five creatures standing, waiting. One strides forward as the platform's bubble recedes and our seats fall away beneath us. As the creature comes closer, I recognize the shape. Like Sax and Bas, but smaller, and its scales are a dull gray. Several flake off in the steps towards us. But the claws on its four arms shine sharp enough.

"Kaishi. I hoped I would see you again," the creature says, and even with the rasping hiss of an Oratus tongue, it's one I know.

Ignos.

"You have a new body," is the first thing I can think of to say.

We step slowly off of the platform into the dark skeleton of the building. Above us, papered window frames filter brown light coming down from the sky, and a dozen open doors along the street let in the noise of the fighting. I smell dust, the twinge of chemicals.

"A host, Kaishi. That's what we call them," Ignos, ever teaching me. "But this one is a failure."

It does seem to be falling apart. Like it's old, or dying. Why would Ignos call that a failure?

"What do you mean?" I ask.

"There's never an end to our conflict. The Amigga aren't going to stop until we're all dead, which means we need to crush them first. To do that, we need better weapons. We need perfect ones." Ignos glances at his claws.

"So you're making Oratus?"

"They're too hard to capture, but take the DNA from the few we have and maybe we can do what the Amigga did, what we've already done to so many other species. What we'll do to you."

"Yeah, enough of this," Viera announces from beside me. "Now that you're not in her head, it's time to do what should've been done long ago."

She draws her miners as the four Flaum guards around Ignos draw theirs. Viera's hands are faster than Flaum claws, and she has the half-second advantage of knowing just what she's going to do. So her lasers hit first, sending a pair of Ignos' guards burning to the ground.

Ignos, though, doesn't sit and watch, but leaps towards me instead.

"You have to give yourself to us," the Sevora hisses as it flies towards me. "The Sevora need you!"

Malo's metal staff catches Ignos in a wide swing as the creature gets close to me, and Malo slams Ignos down into the ground. The Charre warrior is wielding the staff with both hands, and he raises it up, twists the point, and gets ready to stab the parasite that'd shared my mind.

"Malo!" Viera yells as she comes out of a dive, dodging counter-fire from one of the remaining Flaum.

But not both.

The second, last Flaum's aiming at Malo, and it pulls the trigger as the Charre warrior stabs with the staff. The bolt flies true, taking Malo in the chest and sending him stumbling off of Ignos.

Malo falls at my feet. I want to check on him, but the Flaum is moving its miner towards me now, so I fall back on my training and dive forward, scooping up Malo's dropped staff and getting Ignos' much larger body between me and the Flaum.

Another series of lasers flashes around us—Viera, getting back to work.

"This isn't you, Kaishi," Ignos hisses, standing back up, a motion that sheds more scales. "You're not a fighter. You're a leader."

"And what are you, Ignos? I thought you were my friend." I hold the staff ready, watch those claws.

"I never claimed to be anything other than I was. I gave you miracles, the tools you needed to save your people. All I ask in return is a chance, a chance for my own species to survive."

"Not by taking over the very people you helped save!"

"There's no other way!"

Ignos jumps at me after its roar, and I dance back, batting at a claw with the end of the staff. I'd seen Sax and Bas move, and Ignos seems jerky, unsure of how to manage the limbs. Of course, if it's only had the body for a few days . . .

I press the attack. Roll off my back foot and dart into Ignos' reach. The Sevora tries to adjust its long swings—claws slashing to where it thought I'd be, but can't seem to move them fast enough. I drive the center of the staff up and bash into its mouth, then, as Ignos backpedals, bring the staff down to my waist and shove it forward like a spear.

The point sticks into Ignos' side, punching through thin, fragile scales. Sick, thick blood oozes around the wound, and Ignos clutches at the staff, looks at me with those yellow Oratus eyes.

"Perhaps I was wrong," Ignos mutters.

"You were wrong about many things," I reply.

Ignos yanks the staff free, letting more of the body's blood flow, and holds it in its right midclaw.

"There's an advantage to being a host, Kaishi," Ignos says. "You only feel what you want to feel."

The Sevora steps towards me, and then a bright flash comes over my shoulder, strikes Ignos in the Oratus' wide chest, and drops the creature to the ground.

"Come on, Kaishi," Viera says, running up next to me. "The thing was evil anyway."

The lift lands in the Nexus and the five of them exit into a sliding crowd of chaos. Species run back and forth, some alone and others in groups. Some carrying weapons, most looking for places to hide. Asking for escape mods, or how to surrender.

Sax doesn't care to tell them that the Vincere won't take prisoners. Not here, not anymore.

It's a quick sprint through the Nexus to the spoke where the *Mobius* is parked. Even in their various levels of panic, the crowds make way for the hulking Oratus and their heavily-armed friends. More than a few tag along behind them—presumably going for their own ships and figuring to be where the firepower is.

Which proves to be a good decision for everyone when the Sisters announce that the first shuttles have landed.

The docking spoke itself is a long, wide hallway with neon-lit numbers hanging outside large, arched doors leading into the bays themselves. Beneath the numbers are the names of the current occupants, and Sax can see the blazing blue of #6, and beneath it, *Mobius*, far down the spoke.

Most of the bays, though, are empty. And most of their doors are opening.

"Too late," Black says. "Cover?"

Two choices—either they press through, try to make it to the bay, or sit back and fight it out with the coming forces. The problem with the latter is the Vincere has more troops, more weapons than they do.

"If we play it safe, we're dead," Sax announces. "I'll go for your ship, and we'll come back for you. Cover me."

He tosses Bas the miner he still has from the Flaum, then Sax breaks for the wall.

Agra-Red and Plake take up the task of covering fire, along with a bunch of *Scrapper Station* scoundrels, and unleash lasers at the groups of soldiers pouring into the spoke. There's not much to hide behind in the hallway—a few crates here and there, some battery racks that everyone stays well away from, so the firefight quickly degenerates into a blinding murderer's row.

Sax goes up the right wall, using his claws to pull himself along. Space station walls aren't designed to resist Oratus claws, so he slices his way in a rapid scramble towards the soldiers.

Shouts and screams grow loud, then a stray shot strikes something combustible and an explosion rocks the middle of the spoke, smoke and fizzing energy filling the air. Sax can't see anything except the flashes of those not deterred by the fact they can't see their target. He keeps moving forward, keeps his vents closed as long as possible—who knows what terrible gasses are getting blown through the air now.

It's hard to hit an Oratus in perfect conditions, much less when Sax has a wall of gray hiding him from view. Sax climbs over the blue glow of Bay Five, and not long after finds himself above number six. He drops to the ground, is about to head through the doors, when he realizes they're closed.

Sax dashes to the control panel along one side, slams the button to open, but all he gets is a simple error message. Locked. So instead he taps the intercom, tries to talk through.

"Who's calling?" It's Engee, the Teven.

"Sax. Open the bay door."

"Where's Plake?"

Sax hears a noise behind him. The smoke's too thick to see what it is, but this far down the spoke, it's not likely to be a friend.

"She's busy. I need you to help me rescue them."

"How about you tell me where she is, and we'll get them first."

Sax hisses, raises his claw and is about to slam it against the panel, when a miner bolt crashes into the wall next to him.

"Tricked me once, Sax," Gar rasps. "It's not going to happen a second time."

Turning your back on an enemy is the last thing Sax wants to do, especially when that enemy has four sharp claws and a pair of talons. But the *Mobius* has to get in the air, or one of the lasers still flying through the smoke is going to hit Bas.

"Go up to Bay One. They're right outside the door," Sax manages to say before a pair of claws dig into his shoulder and throw him away from the intercom.

"Talking to someone?" Gar hisses, diving on top of Sax, teeth snapping at Sax's throat.

Sax, pushing Gar back with his own foreclaws, manages to get his tail between the two of them and pushes up with the strong muscle. His tail shoves Gar up and off of him, through the air and into the smoke somewhere back up the spoke.

The Oratus hops to a crouch, scans the mist. There's still plenty of battle noise, though he's seeing fewer flashes coming back this way. The little band of roughs was never going to last long.

Gar drops from above, and Sax only gets a split second warning from the sudden curl of the gray smoke. Sax tries to leap right as Gar crashes into him, and that centimeter of distance means Gar's talons only dig a long gash down Sax's neck instead of piercing his head. Without the solid landing, Gar has to catch himself on the ground, which puts him at perfect level for Sax's tail to crack into him.

This time, Sax's smashing blow sends Gar into the Bay Six door, and Sax doesn't let his former friend set himself. Sax bounds forward and, in a single long leap, pins Gar. With his left foreclaw, Sax drives Gar's neck back against the metal, the tips of his claws pressing in on Gar's scales.

"You never did care enough about your surroundings," Sax hisses.

"I'm not the only one," Gar rasps.

A wash of blue light hits Sax, and he feels all sensation drop away, all things fade into a numb nothing.

23 / FIGHT AND FLIGHT

Malo's still on the ground when we turn to him, and he's sporting a deep burn in his chest. His eyes are closed and his breathing comes ragged.

"Can we lift him up?" Viera says, and I move to try.

The warrior isn't light, though, and it takes both of us to even get Malo off the ground. As we lift him, Malo's eyes jerk open and he gasps.

"Don't move me!" Malo says, leaning on us. "It's too painful."

"It's either that or you get to stay here with all these lovely bodies," Viera replies.

"We're not far," I say, though it's only a guess. "It's no worse than when Jakkan's assassins attacked us back home."

Malo closes his eyes tight for a second, then nods.

"One step at a time," I say, and then we move.

Viera keeps one miner drawn in her right hand as we creep forward. I manage to sneak a look at the rest of the Flaum, at the smoke still rising from their bodies.

"You're deadlier than I thought," I say to her.

"Apparently I have to be around you," Viera replies. "Seems we get into all kinds of trouble."

My hand, on Malo's waist, feels his sweat, his shaking skin. I don't know if he's going to make it out of this, but I'm going to do my best to try.

We exit the egg-shaped building and find ourselves on a broad street. Not too far away, I can see the gigantic oval marking the spaceport, the place where we landed after Ignos first tricked us into traveling here.

"It's not far, Malo, not far," I whisper to him.

"Just keep going," Malo replies, his eyes still shut.

So that's what we do. With the continuing chaos throughout the city, nobody bothers stopping to see what's going on with three struggling species moving slow along the ground. We pass beneath huge buildings, under swooping walkways and tubes, many of which still have platforms shuttling people from one place to another. Even an all-out attack from Clarity's Dawn apparently doesn't shut down Vimelia.

"Did you see Ignos?" I ask Viera as we move. "The body it was using seemed like it was falling apart."

"Maybe they only had an old one." Viera doesn't sound the least bit curious. "Or the thing was sick. I'm not complaining, either way."

We carry on for a few more steps. Malo's getting heavier, but I'm not going to leave him, so I dig deep, push through the soreness in my shoulders and the pressure on my back and keep going.

I'm still curious how Ignos managed to grab us, how it redirected the platform to ambush us there at the bottom of the building. If it was planned, why only go with a few Flaum? If it wasn't, how did Ignos find us so fast?

"Kaishi, do you remember when the Emperor died?" Malo says, his voice soft, weaker than I've ever heard it.

"You led our forces. Won the fight."

"I slept," Viera adds. "It was glorious."

"I thought I was doing it for revenge, to honor his sacrifice," Malo continues. "But I think we all knew, even the Emperor, that it wasn't him we were fighting for, but for you and what you were giving us. If we lost you, then we would lose everything."

"You mean, if you lost Ignos," I reply.

"No, you. For whatever else you are, Kaishi, you're kind. You care. If Ignos had found a warrior that didn't hold back, who just wanted to conquer, then we would all have lost."

"Quiet, Malo," I don't want him to die mid-sentence, especially now that we've carried him this far. "Try to save your strength."

"Not like Kaishi needs the praise anyway," Viera says. "She knows she's great."

Malo manages a half laugh, then falls silent again.

The spaceport is larger, closer now. There's no grand entrance, but instead a series of tunnels with arched openings leading down. In front of the closest opening, I see a familiar face and wave my arm.

Rackt and a pair of Clarity's Dawn Whelk scramble over to us and take a look at Malo.

"Can you help him?" I ask the Vyphen, whose packing a trio of miners, one larger in his hands and two smaller ones like Viera's on his belt.

The Vyphen glances at one of the Whelks, who pulls a pack off his gooey back and sets down near Malo, pulling a tube of some fluid and spreading a clear liquid over the area of the burn.

"It's a bad one," the Whelk says as he spreads the gel. "He needs better help than we can give him here."

Then the Whelk pulls something out of his pack—a little jar that I recognize.

"Stim?" I say as the Whelk sticks a needle through the rubber lid of the jar, pulls it back out coated in the sticky stuff.

"You've seen it?" Rackt asks.

"I've used it," I reply. "If we live through this, I'll tell you about it."

"Speaking of," Viera's eyes are tracking behind us, and while the Whelk gives Malo a dose of the energizing drug, we see a shuttle lift off from back the way we came, near the egg structure.

The craft wobbles in the air, then tilts its nose down and begins to speed towards us.

"What do you want to bet that's Ignos?" Viera says.

"No deal," I reply. "Let's get out of here."

I turn, and help a suddenly awake Malo to his feet. The Whelk throws his medical pack around his body and then we start to scramble for the entrance. My feet hit hard on the tile, and I feel Malo's hand tight in mine as we go.

"This, what I'm feeling, isn't natural," he says as we run.

"It's saving your life," I reply. "Don't complain."

"Not complaining, just surprised."

The entryway looms before us, an arch with a glowing red frame dotted with those black nodules. The ones I've come to realize can let others see you from far away.

Yet another thing I'll be glad to leave behind on this rotten world.

A gradual roar grows behind us and I don't have to look to know it's the shuttle. Air pushes us forward faster, and we make it past the threshold, the beige sky getting replaced by brighter, unnatural white lights. Which flicker as that rumbling roar gets so loud, so close—

"It's crashing!" Viera yells. "Dive!"

And we do as everything collapses, burns and explodes around us.

Somewhere in the tumble I lose track of Malo's hand. We're rolling through falling rock, bouncing down the slope until, finally hitting the bottom, I roll to a rest.

The mask keeps me upright and uncut, though it does nothing about the bruises and twisted ankle I'm feeling after that roll. Still, I'm the first one up, and I'm staring back at the collapsed entry and seeing carnage.

The front nose of the shuttle, gray and shattered now, is nearly touching me. Its wings are gone, and behind and around it, the entire tunnel has collapsed. Stone, sparking lights, and an unknown amount of pipes are bent and bursting around the craft.

The bodies of my friends, of Rackt and the medic Whelk—I don't see the other—are scattered around me. They're mostly still, or moaning. There's a sharp hiss, and the front of the shuttle, the glass shield, pops off and falls aside to the ground. Climbing out, its claws scraping against the side as it drops down, is Ignos.

Its Oratus body is bleeding from everywhere. There's a black scoring on its chest from Viera's blast, and the deep gouge from the staff looks like it hasn't sealed. Yet Ignos is standing there, staring at me with an open mouth full of razor teeth.

"Sevora can push past the pain, Kaishi," Ignos hisses at me. "We can bring a body to heights it could never achieve otherwise."

I'm shaking my head, even as I hope my friends can get themselves up. "You're killing it."

"This one? This one never really lived in the first place. From a tube to being my host, it wouldn't know what to do with freedom if it ever tasted it." Ignos steps towards me, its claws clacking against the docking bay's floor.

"That shouldn't be your choice to make."

"Yes. I could have left you alone. Let your tribe, all your people die in the name of freedom," Ignos doesn't stop. "Instead, I saved you. You owe me a debt, Kaishi. One you can repay right now by coming with me. Joining me."

"To do what, Ignos?" I cry. "What can I do that your Oratus body can't?"

"Save my species!" Ignos lunges forward with the last word, and I try to back-step.

Even with the mask, I'm not quick enough. Even weakened, the Oratus has too much strength. Ignos catches me, whips its tail behind my legs and trips me onto the ground.

It looms over me, and for a moment there in its yellow-black eyes I see something other than malice. And I reach for it.

"You don't want to kill me," I try to say.

"I don't," Ignos replies. "Yet, if you won't come willingly, then I have no choice."

"But if you hurt me, hurt us, you won't get what you want?"

"Look at this." Ignos flexes its claws. "It's not perfect, but it's close enough. And with time, we'll perfect it. I don't need you alive to get what I want."

Ignos raises its right foreclaw, and then it's no longer on top of me. There's a flash, and I see a mad ball of limbs. Black hair that I recognize.

Malo. His fists are flying, and connecting, until Ignos gets a claw into the man's back, bites in and flings Malo off of him and into the smooth docking-bay wall.

In the moment between Malo hitting the wall and Ignos getting back up, I realize we're far from the only people in the spaceport. Behind us, farther into the vast space, plenty of craft are coming and going. Their punctuating rockets add a peppered background noise to the continuing rumbles of far-off demolitions and the closer fizzle of sparking pipes.

There's bystanders too—species I'm assuming are controlled by Sevora, Flaum and others, staring at us from a safe distance.

An audience that scatters as soon as Viera gets up to a crouch and sends a few warning shots their way. Sends one over at Ignos too, which hits just over its ducking head.

"Gotta run, Kaishi," Viera curses as she half-walks, half stumbles over to me.

"We can't leave Malo," I reply, though I'm weaponless.

"No problem, you get the warrior, I'll take care of the slug." Viera raises the miner and advances on Ignos.

But she doesn't get there. One of those shuttles I assumed was leaving the spaceport zooms towards us, blasts over the heads of the fleeing spectators and clomps its gear down next to me. The shuttle's shaped like a diamond, with the massive rockets glaring out one end of a smooth, pinkish shell.

"You all better get in here right now, or you're going to lose your ride!" T'Oli's voice, blasting out over the speakers. "Sapphrite told me to get you off this rock, but it didn't say I had to kill myself to do it, so you've got one chance!"

"Have one thing to take care of!" I shout back towards the ship, though I have no idea if T'Oli can hear me.

In any case, I run towards Malo's limp form. I'm not leaving him.

Ignos, with Viera working towards him, turns and runs. The battered body can still move with all six claws and talons pushing in concert. Viera tries a shot, misses left as Ignos juts beneath a resting spacecraft and keeps going.

I'm getting close to Malo, calling his name, and I don't like that he's not moving. There's a chill starting in my spine that I don't like, a reality growing I refuse to acknowledge.

He's a meter away when a bright flash splits the docking area, lancing ahead of me into the wall and shattering the rock. It's followed by a second shot, a red color, that slags the floor in front of me, turns the metal floor into molten soup.

"They won't miss a second time!" T'Oli calls.

"Kaishi!" Viera yells, heading towards T'Oli's ship. "Get him and go!"

I jump over the damaged floor, then dive towards Malo as another flash lights up the world ahead of me. Strikes the wall where Malo's lying, blasting rocks, metal, and worse all over him.

I start to scramble forward when pink metal slides in front of me, cutting me off from Malo's body. A door is open in the bottom of the craft, a thin ramp sliding down from it. My right foot plants and I jump, getting over the ramp and heading right towards Malo's body when something catches me, grabs hold of the robe I'm still wearing and pulls me back onto the ramp.

"You can't save him, Kaishi," Viera says, pulling me up the ramp.

"We can! He's right there!" But even as I say the words, I feel the pink shuttle shake as the Sevora defense pours their next attack into it.

"Malo gave himself for you, Empress, don't let it be for nothing," Viera says, and in that moment I stop fighting her.

I'm not stupid—going down for Malo means killing T'Oli, Viera, all of us. So I turn, I turn away from the warrior that'd stood by me for so long and leave him to die.

No connection. He's in a void. No, there's something. A spark. He can hold onto it. Push.

Harder.

Sax manages to open his eyes a narrow slit. It's barely enough to see.

But he has to start somewhere.

There's netting all around him. A forest of it. He must be in one of the shuttles, which explains the line of terminals in front, and the pair of Oratus working them. The cockpit window shows pure black space. Stars. The occasional laser flash arcing past them into oblivion.

Sax should feel the vibration from the engines, but he can't. Should be able to taste the tang of recycled air, but his vents now operate on instinct alone, on reflexive nerve action. No conscious thought required.

His mouth doesn't work either.

This must be what the Sevora feel like in a human's brain.

Gar twists his head around, looks at Sax. Spreads a toothy grin, "Looks like our friend is waking up."

Lan twitches her own head around, then snaps it back forward. To the terminals, the radars and flight controls.

"Stun him if he moves."

"His legs and arms are clasped." Gar shrugs. "He's not going anywhere. Though I suppose I could take a few bites if we want to be sure."

"Until they prove he's helping Evva, Sax is still Vincere. We shouldn't hurt him more than we have to."

"Sounds like a gray area to me."

Lan doesn't bother fighting further, which is like her. Keep Gar from going too far, but letting him go far enough. Sax tries to get more control, tries to find his own nerves as Gar steps away from the terminals. Heads over to him.

"We're almost to the frigate," Gar rasps as he squats down near Sax. "Don't know where Bas went. Didn't think she'd abandon you, but we always thought you two were a strange pairing. Maybe she's taking her chance."

Sax tries to glare. Only succeeds in closing his eyes enough for everything to go hazy gray.

"Don't like that thought? You'll have plenty of time to stew on it. The Amigga'll roast you for a good long while, make sure to get every useful morsel out of you." Gar wiggles his claws in front of Sax. "Then what do you do with a good weapon gone bad? I'll suggest a few things."

Something causes the shuttle to shake, because Gar suddenly leans to the side, sweeps out with his tail to stabilize himself.

"What's happening out there?" Gar looks back at Lan.

"We're being chased." Lan replies.

"Obviously. By who?"

"I don't know, but I can guess."

Sax manages to push his eyes open and sees Lan swing the shuttle to the right, replacing the star field with the solid pearl-white shape of the frigate. It's a beautiful, ridged feather of a craft, with sharp edges fanning out to provide the many docking points for fighters, shuttles, and other ships. A vessel Sax would have been proud to serve on, not long ago.

One that, if he lands on it now, will mean his death.

Getting hit with a stunning miner is like receiving a massive shock. The blast overloads the nerves, fries their connections and leaves them in a withered state, unable to send information until they recover. Depending on the shot—Sax is sure this came from a heavier miner than the one Lan used earlier—and the shielding—Sax wasn't wearing a full mask—the stun could work for hours or minutes.

There's another factor, one harder to quantify—will. Need. Desire. Sax can't make his nerves heal faster, but he can try to push movements through to his muscles. He can tell his claws to clench, his mouth to bite, his tail to swish, and while none of these get through intact, the Oratus starts to twitch.

Which gets Gar moving to the weapons rack—a literal spot to store miners against the wall while the shuttle's in motion. Sax can't turn his head enough to see what Gar's grabbing, but he's thinking he has a couple of seconds until his world goes black again.

Gar comes back into view. Aims the miner directly at Sax's chest.

"They say this doesn't damage muscles," Gar rasps. "Only the nerves. Not that it matters for you."

The shuttle rocks again. A warning light blinks on and loud ringing tones fill the cockpit.

"Thought you could fly one of these things?" Gar yells, looking back over his shoulder.

Sax pushes harder. His tail swishes.

"This isn't a fighter!" Lan replies.

Gar shakes his scaly head, turns back to Sax, then seems to get an idea. "Lan, open up a line to'em. Tell them if they hit us again, Sax dies."

"The Amigga won't like that!"

"We'll be dead, so it doesn't matter!"

Sax has to agree with Gar on that one. The conversation, though, is buying him a bit of time. More swishes. His eyes are fully open now. The air tastes stale—not much of it in here, but the fact that Sax gets any flavor at all is good.

"All right," Gar raises the miner again. "Time to sleep."

Sax sees Gar's claw depress the trigger, and Sax puts all his effort into one thing: a roll. His back shifts, his claws and talons, clasped together, swing Sax back into the netting, which sags deeper into the shuttle. And Gar's shot, a blinding bright blue, strikes right where Sax should have been.

Then the net rebounds, pushes Sax back to his spot.

"Nice try." Gar glances at the miner, confirms its still got energy. Raises it again.

"Gar!" Lan shouts suddenly. "They're—"

And the rest of her words vanish as the shuttle's roof cracks and breaks apart.

The ceiling over Sax's head shifts from its boring light gray to a red, then orange and white color. Pieces of the structure start to fall and again Sax pushes himself to roll away from the liquid drops of molten metal. Gar dances back too, forgetting about his captive and aiming the miner towards where the hole is forming.

Towards where, as the shuttle's hull peels back, Agra-Red's manic, helmeted face shows. Just behind the Whelk is the billowing beige of a docking tube, one that must be sealed against the shuttle's non-melted hull. Necessary to keep everyone from being sucked away in the vacuum.

Sax briefly wonders why Plake's ship would have the equipment necessary for this kind of raid, files it away under things to consider when he's not in a life-threatening fight, and resumes kicking and pushing himself along the net towards the shuttle's side.

"Give it up, Gar! Lan!" Bas' rasping shout rings into the shuttle. "You're trapped. Surrender, and you'll leave with your lives!"

"They're countering the thrust," Lan says to Gar. "The shuttle's engines aren't strong enough to keep us going forward."

"Tell the frigate to blast them off." Gar aims the miner through the hole, but doesn't pull the trigger. If Gar breaks apart the tunnel, Sax and everyone else will be sucked into space. For once, the Oratus shows restraint.

"And chance that they'll hit us?" Lan says. "I'm radioing the fighters. They'll be better."

"Anyone shoots at us, and we'll blow your ship," Bas says, still not trying to come down through the hole.

Their threats continue back and forth while Sax works at his bindings. They're hard clasps, energized iron. He can't get his tail around for leverage, but there's something he does have, something designed to get through just about anything.

Teeth.

Sax brings his claw clasps up to his mouth as Gar shouts something back at Bas. Slips the thin edge of the circle tight on his right foreclaw past his lip, and nibbles. Feels the points of his teeth echo pain, but he tastes metal too. Progress.

He's most of the way through the link—and Sax's teeth are grinding down—when Gar ups the risk.

"If you come down through there, Lan's going to blow the shuttle. Or I will," Gar hisses. "We're not going to lose. Either allow us to land, or we'll all going to die."

Sax isn't sure how Gar thinks it's possible for the shuttle to dock now that there's a hole in its ceiling, but Gar's true meaning is clear; they're not surrendering.

"Lan," Bas shouts. "You know this isn't right! You know we're not the enemy!"

Lan, still by the controls, doesn't respond. Instead, she's tapping away at something. Sax doesn't know what, but the sooner he can free

. . .

There. The clasp doesn't spring loose, exactly, but the strength holding it together, keeping Sax's right foreclaw from slipping out, vanishes. Sax, though, keeps still for a second. Makes sure Gar's attention is still on the tunnel, on the potential attack from the *Mobius*.

Then Sax slips his claw free and, using its razor points, skewers the central control box keeping the clasps together. They drop off, and in the same motion, Sax swings his legs up and frees those too.

The stun isn't all gone, so getting up feels a little like a dream—Sax can't feel every nerve ending, and only knows his muscles are doing what he wants them to by what he can see—namely that Gar and his miner are at eye-level now.

And Gar doesn't miss Sax's move either. The Oratus audibly growls, swings the miner towards Sax.

"Too late," Sax says.

Gar's about to reply when a bolt lances down through the hole. Blue and bright, burying itself into Gar's shoulder. It's followed by a second and third, putting the Oratus down hard. Sax walks over to the paralyzed body of his former friend, snags Gar's miner off the floor of the shuttle and aims it at Lan.

"Step away from the terminals," Sax says to Lan. "Choose. Now. It's us, or them."

Lan looks at Gar. "We're not perfect, but we're loyal, Sax. To the cause, not to any one commander."

"I don't think there is a cause, Lan," Sax hisses back. "It's only what the Amigga want. You're a pawn in their game."

"Maybe that's what we're supposed to be," Lan replies. Then she points at a hatch towards the back of the shuttle. The craft's sole escape mod. "We'll go that way."

Sax flips the miner's switch without thinking, changes it from stun to kill. Every bit of instinct is telling him not to leave these two alive. Not to give them another chance.

"If you take him, if you leave," Sax starts.

"Next time, there's no mercy." Lan picks Gar up from the shuttle's floor, and heads to the escape mod. Taps at the panel with her tail to open the door. "Sax, you're choosing the wrong side."

"I'm making a choice, Lan, which is more than what the Amigga will ever let you do."

Lan does nothing more than nod, then she slips inside with her pair, seals the door, and blasts away.

Bas drops into the shuttle after Sax announces the all-clear, and she helps her pair head back up, through the short docking tunnel to the *Mobius*. Disconnecting the boarding seal involves the same superheating method—after Agra-Red seals off the tunnel behind a hatch, a gout of energy melts away the seal and the tunnel retracts.

And Plake immediately sends the *Mobius* into a spiraling whirl.

"Fighters, lasers, they're all coming!" the Vyphen captain shouts over the ship's broadcast system.

With both Lan and Gar free and away, the frigate and the fighters have no reason to be cautious, and apparently any information Sax and Bas have isn't worth letting them get away alive.

"Turrets?" Sax asks Agra-Red as the Whelk moves towards the front of the ship.

"None made for you," Agra-Red says, sliding onto the platform and riding it to the *Mobius'* second level. "Oratus are too large, too ugly for our guns."

"Too ugly?" Bas says, but the Whelk's already slipped away into a gunnery hatch.

"Funny, coming from a Whelk," Sax rasps.

The two of them head up to the bridge, where Plake is busy guiding the *Mobius* through one dive and twist after another. Sax and Bas grab onto some crash netting and watch while the universe spins and slides. Laser fire flashes around them, and the *Mobius* rattles as shots find their mark.

"Leap away!" Sax says.

"If I stay still for a second, we'll be burned to ash," Plake shouts back, slipping the ship into a dive back towards *Scrapper Station*.

Sax gets a proud moment when he sees *Scrapper Station*'s still sending hot energy out at the Vincere's fighters and retreating shuttles.

Retreating.

"We actually drove them off?" Sax says.

Plake laughs and Bas shakes her head. "They only wanted us. After they realized you'd been captured and I was on this ship, after Engee crashed it through Bay One, they started to retreat."

"But the station will survive?"

"Sentimental, Sax?" Bas says. "I didn't think you cared for it."

Plake guides the *Mobius* beneath *Scrapper Station*, using its spokes as barriers to block the fire. There's less of that too, now that they're out of the frigate's range. Sax begins to think they might make it out of this one alive.

"They don't deserve to die for us," Sax replies.

Though even as he says the words, Sax knows he'd give all of *Scrapper Station* up for their cause over and over again. And as Plake sets the *Mobius* in a level line, looking to leap, he knows they might have to.

"Where are we going?" Sax asks as the short countdown appears on the cockpit glass.

"A place to hide," Plake says. "So we can figure out how to find your friend."

Then the stars bend and warp, like Sax does himself, and they're gone.

As T'Oli careens out of the spaceport, I get one last look at the bodies of Rackt, the Whelk that escaped the crash, and even Ignos, whose Oratus form is bearing a pair of new blast wounds.

"You shot Ignos?" I ask Viera, numbly, who's standing behind me while the boarding ramp closes.

"It tried to kill you. It killed Malo. It deserved to die, Kaishi." Viera turns away from me and walks back into the shuttle.

I follow her, taking a glazed look over the room we've entered. The gray-metal walls and ceiling look like the very first spaceship ride I took with the Oratus where they'd kept us tied up in the back. Where we'd suffered through a leap among boxes and boxes of nutrient goop.

There aren't many crates here, though—instead, there's a number of wide creamy circles that, when we approach, grow out furniture to match our bodies. Chairs, couches, and small tables.

It's too much, and I've no interest in sitting down anyway.

"I'm going up," I tell Viera, who collapses onto one of the couches and doesn't appear the least bit interested in what I'm doing.

Up, in this shuttle, means a wide pearl stair with dual bronze hand-rails that, as soon as I hit the first step, shift to match the height of my hands. I don't think I'm going to need them until the shuttle shakes again, throwing me to the side and forcing me to grip tight to one of the railings or be thrown back towards Viera.

"I'd sit down, cause these Sevora don't seem to want to let us go."

T'Oli's order is enough to push me up the stairs. I'm not going to wait for death—like Malo, I'm going to face it. See what's going to end me. So I press my legs down and power up the steps between volleys, get forward to a narrow cockpit that must be in the shuttle's pinkish nose. T'Oli's spread itself around the various switches and knobs, so that it looks like the whole control panel is covered in a white plaster.

"Thought I said to sit down?" T'Oli's sole fluid patch, with its pair of eye stalks, flaps at me.

"I'm not," I state. "Are we going to make it?"

"Depends," T'Oli says, "on whether they can shoot straight."

From the cockpit, I can see the rapidly-approaching edge of space. The beige sky is fading towards a deep blue and then black. T'Oli keeps the shuttle weaving, so that the view jerks and twists as we fly. Flashes punctuate the movements; lasers biting off into the space beyond us. Which, I realize, is far from empty. Even up here, hordes of Sevora shuttles and other ships blaze around like wasps, heading who knows where.

"They're all panicked because Sapphrite's broadcasting Vimelia's location to the galaxy right now," T'Oli says, and I'm stunned at how calm the Ooblot is. "Going to gather up their things, I bet, and make a run for it. They'll have to hope the Chorus doesn't have anything nearby to catch the signal."

"How long will they have?" The opportunity to talk about something so pointless and unrelated to what just happened is, somehow, necessary.

"Depends. You assume nobody gets away, assume that the Chorus has nobody in any neighboring systems, and you've got a long time." T'Oli laughs, then. "But then, you've also got us."

The shuttle rocks again, and I think I hear T'Oli issue some sort of Ooblot curse, which sounds like a mix between scraping rocks and gnashing teeth.

"Sorry 'bout that," T'Oli says. "Got a little distracted."

I decide maybe being quiet till we're out of danger is a good plan, and when T'Oli mentions that we'll be leaping in a few moments, I take the hint and go back down. Viera's still staring silent into a vague distance, so I take a seat and drift.

I first met Malo when he appeared at the base of my village's temple to Ignos, our Tier. He tore me away from my family, from the life I'd known every waking day to that point, and declared that I could be the one to lead his people. He'd had confidence in me from that very first moment. Believed that I could do great things, and when I'd needed his help, Malo had done what I asked without hesitation.

Somewhere during those thoughts, T'Oli pops the shuttle into a leap. Like with the others, I'm twisted, turned, folded and frayed, but through it all I keep Malo's face in focus and run through our memories.

"Kaishi," Viera's voice jars me out of the reverie. "I need you here. Now."

I blink. We'd just come out of our leap, and T'Oli hadn't said anything yet. What did Viera need?

Around us, the shuttle's glossy white furniture sits sterile and dull. On the ceiling the walls have faded to a translucence that gives easy vision to the dark space and sparkling stars. I'd call it beautiful if the word could come anywhere near my lips at the moment.

"Malo didn't attack Ignos so you could mope," Viera says, though the red around her eyes says she's been doing some of her own moping during our journey home.

"He didn't need to," I reply. "Ignos wouldn't have killed me. Not if I'd gone along with it."

"Which wasn't an option."

"Wasn't it, though? I'd already had a Sevora inside my head. I know how to control them. You both could have escaped."

"We wouldn't have left you," Viera sighs as she says this. "Because, stupid people that we are, we both agreed to get you back. We swore ourselves to you."

"Like you can't break that oath."

"Kaishi, everything's changed. I don't know what's happening anymore. Sometimes I think the only way I'm holding on is precisely because of that oath, so don't take it away from me."

"As if I'm worth protecting anyway." I glance down at my hands. The ones that couldn't even save my most cherished friend.

"Stop it." Viera's annoyed now. "No Empress gets to talk like that."

She's right. I know she is. I take a big breath, shudder out the exhale, and look over at those stairs. Time to go and see where T'Oli's taken us.

"Sorry, Kaishi, but it looks like we're a little late," T'Oli cheerfully announces as I join it in the cockpit. "You see all those shapes around your planet?"

Earth, in its sparkling blue beauty, appears marred by a dozen dark gashes cutting across its surface.

"Those are Sevora ships. My guess is they took the coordinates off of whatever shuttle you rode to Vimelia."

"They can't have been here too long, though," I reply. "We didn't stay on Vimelia more than a few days!"

"If you're lucky, that means they'll only control *most* of the planet by now," T'Oli quips. "Anyway, seeing as your home's a loss, where should we go? Rackt and some of the others were supposed to have a plan, but they, uh, didn't look too alive when we left."

"We're not going anywhere." There isn't any question of that now. "Take us down, T'Oli. Take me home."

"Might not be your home anymore, Kaishi."

"Then I'll take it back."

. . .

Read on for an excerpt from Creator's End the Skyward Saga book four, or find more adventures with Black Key Books:

Criminal. Rebel. Fighter.

Traitor.

Useless words. Unable to capture the depth of feeling swarming through Sax as he stands, with Bas, on the bridge of the *Mobius*. Plake herself is at the controls, her skin only visible on her head, with everything else covered by rainbow feathers. She's orienting the *Mobius* now, pointing it towards a mustard-yellow planet whose surface swirls with passing storms.

"This is your idea of a place to hide?" Bas asks as the planet comes into view. "Rathfall?"

"When was the last time you heard of the Vincere coming here?" Plake replies, that burble of hers tickling Sax's ears.

Vyphen always sound like they're underwater.

"Rathfall won't have what we need." Sax flexes his claws. They're still not moving perfectly, and he's worried the heavy stunning might have done some permanent damage. "Evva won't be here, and we won't be able to find passage to the Chorus this far on the outer edges."

"The Chorus?" Plake laughs, then turns to the red slug-like creature at the back of the bridge, the eternally armed Agra-Red. "You hear them? They're traitors and they want to go to the Chorus!"

"I think it's true—Oratus without the Vincere just want to die," the Whelk says.

"That's—" Sax can't finish the words before a buzzing alarm cuts him off.

The sound's the same no matter the ship. A signal to find your crash netting and get situated, because you're about to hit atmosphere and going from zero air to lots of it makes for a bumpy ride. None of them have to move far; panels in the ceiling above them pop open and the black, padded stripes fall down to connect with magnetic loops in the floor. Making himself safe is as easy as falling backwards and getting caught.

Sax doesn't bother restarting the conversation, because it's too late. The view outside is entirely swirling yellows now, and the *Mobius* is already rattling in its descent. Plake wouldn't change course this deep. After they land, Sax and Bas will have to find another way off-world, back to where they need to be.

Entering Rathfall's atmosphere is a visual treat, once Sax decides the *Mobius* is well-built enough to handle the turbulence. The planet is the product of hyper-pollinating plants and the giant, mindless insects that swarm from each flower to the next, scattering so much of the pollen that the planet's covered in the stuff. Ordinarily, the shading of starlight would have resulted in a super-cooled atmosphere, but the plants dealt with their own problem, burrowing deep into Rathfall's soil and rock to release heat from the planet's core.

The plant's practice was quickly co-opted and refined by those who found Rathfall's natural cover a perfect opportunity for businesses the Amigga didn't want in the open. With guidance, the plants now keep Rathfall's temperature equalized, and with that balance, trade flourishes.

Outside, the pollen scatters and bursts as the *Mobius* plows through pockets. Some sticks to the windshield for a second, exploding out against the pressure in grainy-yellow patterns. Flames appear as the ship hits the harder parts of the atmosphere, flicking in whites and blues along the edges of the glass. Sax thinks he can make out larger shadows flitting in the distance—the bugs about their work.

When they get beneath the upper pollen cloud, into the pocket of pressure that splits Rathfall's canopy with its floor, it's as if the *Mobius* is suspended for a moment in between worlds. Sax can see clear to the left and the right, with the windy tendrils of pollen above and the roiling, thicker mass of it below.

Plake pulls the *Mobius* out of its dive and settles into a streak across the surface, heading towards, Sax has no doubt, one of the Spires.

"What will you do?" Bas asks now that the rough-and-tumble part of the entry is over. "Leave us and run?"

"You promised me a way to get back at the Amigga," Plake doesn't hesitate before replying. "We're seeing it through. I want those ugly things knocked down as much as you do."

"So you trust us."

"I trust what I can see," Plake replies. "The Vincere want you dead, which means there must be a reason. You two aren't smart enough to be thieves, so my guess is that you're a threat."

"We are always a threat," Sax says.

"Yeah, yeah," Plake sticks up one feathered arm, waves away Sax's words without looking at him. "I get it. The posturing. Oratus always have to be the deadliest ones in the room."

"Even when they're not," Agra-Red says from the back.

On the edge of the horizon, a dark pole appears, jutting up from the clouds beneath and its wide, flat top stopping well below the upper canopy.

Sax pushes away tempting thoughts of carving Agra-Red to fine, jelly bits and instead focuses on Plake.

"So you will not take us to the Chorus, even to hurt the Amigga?" Sax asks.

"Prove to me that's what we need to do and I'll think about it,"

Plake replies. "As it is, we're low on cash and I've still got all these supplies. You failed hard in that respect, Sax."

"Not our fault," Bas replies.

"Guess who doesn't care." Plake ruffles her feathers, then her long tongue wicks out of her mouth and brushes a few of them that didn't fall back into place. "Here's the plan. We'll dig around on Astre's Spire for a bit, see if we can't find out something on your missing commander. Agra-Red'll sell the supplies and Engee can make sure this ship isn't going to fall apart after the hits we took getting away from *Scrapper Station*."

"We're not much good at digging," Sax says. "It's not, as you say, what Oratus are for."

"Oh, I know," Plake replies. "That's why you'll be staying on board. Guard the ship, so that when Coorvin and I figure out where to go, it'll still be around."

"Guard it from what?"

Scrapper Station was lawless enough. How all these places continue to exist on their own, without the Vincere enforcing basic rules, makes no sense to Sax. Then again, if guarding the ship means he can spend the time threatening smaller, more pathetic species, he'll at least be entertained.

"How should I know?" Plake presses a hand on the terminal to her right and, immediately, the windshield covers the visible area around the growing Spire with diagrams, statistics, and news. "Read up, everyone, because in ten more minutes, this is going to be our new home."

Landing in Astre's Spire means doing some light dodging around the mess of cargo drones coming and going, ferrying raw materials to much larger ships that would break apart if they attempted to enter the atmosphere. Plake doesn't seem the slightest bit concerned as she weaves around the blocks and their big engines, and she settles the *Mobius* in with a half-dozen other passenger craft. Almost immediately after, the captain and her crew disembark, leaving Sax and Bas alone with Engee, the Teven who prefers her endless experiments and her lab to interacting with the two Oratus.

At first, it's annoying being left behind. Sax burns to move, to get *going* after being stuck for so long. After an hour of watching ships come and go, and waving off the occasional robot asking if they have cargo to sell, Sax finds himself settling in, finds himself falling into a long conversation with Bas as the two of them stand at the base of the *Mobius'* entrance ramp. It's the first time in a long time they've been able to just be with each other for hours, and the time begins to whirl by as they walk back their memories.

Yet even when Rathfall goes through its deep night, with Astre's Spire lighting itself up in a bright blue glow to be more visible against the yellow murk, there's no sign of Plake, no sign of Agra-Red or Silver and Black, the two Flaum that vanished with them.

Continue the adventure with Creator's End the Skyward Saga Book Four. Thanks for reading!

ACKNOWLEDGMENTS

This novel is the product of my family and friends refusing to let a dream die. My wife Nicole, for letting me write in the early mornings and making sure I didn't starve. My brothers and parents for their continual comments, support, and enthusiasm.

And, of course, you, the reader, for giving me a reason to write.

A.R. Knight spins stories in a frosty house in Madison, WI, primarily owned by a pair of cats. After getting sucked into the working grind in the economic crash of the 2008, he found himself spending boring meetings soaring through space and going on grand adventures.

Eventually, spending time with podcasting, screenplays, short stories and other novels, he found a story he could fall into and a cast of characters both entertaining and full of heart.

From there, A.R. Knight plans on jumping through to other worlds and finding new stories to tell in the limitless borders of our imagination.

Thanks, as always, for reading!

For more information:
www.adamrknight.com

To Clyde and Emma